3 2355 00356479 6

KF 9409 .P65 2010

Political corruption

Oakland Community College
Highland Lakes Library
7350 Cooley Lake Road
Waterford, MI 48327

5/10

DEMCO

Political Corruption

Other Books in the Issues on Trial Series:

Political Corruption

Mitchell Young, Book Editor

GREENHAVEN PRESS

A part of Gale, Cengage Learning

Detroit • New York • San Francisco • New Haven, Conn • Waterville, Maine • London

KF 9409 .P65 2010

Political corruption

38.50

Christine Nasso, *Publisher*
Elizabeth Des Chenes, *Managing Editor*

© 2010 Greenhaven Press, a part of Gale, Cengage Learning

For more information, contact:
Greenhaven Press
27500 Drake Rd.
Farmington Hills, MI 48331-3535
Or you can visit our Internet site at gale.cengage.com.

ALL RIGHTS RESERVED
No part of this work covered by the copyright herein may be reproduced, transmitted, stored, or used in any form or by any means graphic, electronic, or mechanical, including but not limited to photocopying, recording, scanning, digitizing, taping, Web distribution, information networks, or information storage retrieval systems, except as permitted under Section 107 or 108 of the 1976 United States Copyright Act, without the prior written permission of the publisher.

For product information and technology assistance, contact us at

Gale Customer Support, 1-800-877-4253
For permission to use material from this text or product, submit all requests online at
www.cengage.com/permissions

Further permissions questions can be emailed to permissionrequest@cengage.com

Articles in Greenhaven Press anthologies are often edited for length to meet page requirements. In addition, original titles of these works are changed to clearly present the main thesis and to explicitly indicate the author's opinion. Every effort is made to ensure that Greenhaven Press accurately reflects the original intent of the authors. Every effort has been made to trace the owners of copyrighted material.

Cover photograph reproduced by permission of MPI/Hulton Archive/Getty Images.

LIBRARY OF CONGRESS CATALOGING-IN-PUBLICATION DATA

Political corruption / Mitchell Young, book editor.
   p. cm. -- (Issues on trial)
   Includes bibliographical references and index.
   ISBN-13: 978-0-7377-3981-7 (hardcover)
   1. Political corruption--United States--Juvenile literature. I. Young, Mitchell.
   KF9409.P65 2009
   345.73'02323--dc22

                                                                        2009020988

Printed in the United States of America
1 2 3 4 5 6 7 13 12 11 10 09

Contents

Chapter 1: Political Corruption and the Abuse of Executive Privilege

Chapter 2: The Independent Counsel as a Tool Against Corruption

Chapter 3: Fighting Corruption
by Limiting Campaign Spending
and Contributions

Chapter 4: Expanding the Federal Government's Right to Prosecute Local Corruption

Foreword

The U.S. courts have long served as a battleground for the most highly charged and contentious issues of the time. Divisive matters are often brought into the legal system by activists who feel strongly for their cause and demand an official resolution. Indeed, subjects that give rise to intense emotions or involve closely held religious or moral beliefs lay at the heart of the most polemical court rulings in history. One such case was *Brown v. Board of Education* (1954), which ended racial segregation in schools. Prior to *Brown*, the courts had held that blacks could be forced to use separate facilities as long as these facilities were equal to that of whites.

For years many groups had opposed segregation based on religious, moral, and legal grounds. Educators produced heartfelt testimony that segregated schooling greatly disadvantaged black children. They noted that in comparison to whites, blacks received a substandard education in deplorable conditions. Religious leaders such as Martin Luther King Jr. preached that the harsh treatment of blacks was immoral and unjust. Many involved in civil rights law, such as Thurgood Marshall, called for equal protection of all people under the law, as their study of the Constitution had indicated that segregation was illegal and un-American. Whatever their motivation for ending the practice, and despite the threats they received from segregationists, these ardent activists remained unwavering in their cause.

Those fighting against the integration of schools were mainly white southerners who did not believe that whites and blacks should intermingle. Blacks were subordinate to whites, they maintained, and society had to resist any attempt to break down strict color lines. Some white southerners charged that segregated schooling was *not* hindering blacks' education. For example, Virginia attorney general J. Lindsay Almond asserted, "With the help and the sympathy and the love and respect of the white people of the South, the colored man has risen under that educational process to a place of eminence and respect throughout the nation. It has served him well." So when the Supreme Court ruled against the segregationists in *Brown*, the South responded with vociferous cries of protest. Even government leaders criticized the decision. The governor of Arkansas, Orval Faubus, stated that he would not "be a party to any attempt to force acceptance of change to which the people are so overwhelmingly opposed." Indeed, resistance to integration was so great that when black students arrived at the formerly all-white Central High School in Arkansas, federal troops had to be dispatched to quell a threatening mob of protesters.

Nevertheless, the *Brown* decision was enforced and the South integrated its schools. In this instance, the Court, while not settling the issue to everyone's satisfaction, functioned as an instrument of progress by forcing a major social change. Historian David Halberstam observes that the *Brown* ruling "deprived segregationist practices of their moral legitimacy.... It was therefore perhaps the single most important moment of the decade, the moment that separated the old order from the new and helped create the tumultuous era just arriving." Considered one of the most important victories for civil rights, *Brown* paved the way for challenges to racial segregation in many areas, including on public buses and in restaurants.

In examining *Brown*, it becomes apparent that the courts play an influential role—and face an arduous challenge—in shaping the debate over emotionally charged social issues. Judges must balance competing interests, keeping in mind the high stakes and intense emotions on both sides. As exemplified by *Brown*, judicial decisions often upset the status quo and initiate significant changes in society. Greenhaven Press's Issues on Trial series captures the controversy surrounding influential court rulings and explores the social ramifications of such decisions from varying perspectives. Each anthology highlights one social issue—such as the death penalty, students' rights, or wartime civil liberties. Each volume then focuses on key historical and contemporary court cases that helped mold the issue as we know it today. The books include a compendium of primary sources—court rulings, dissents, and immediate reactions to the rulings—as well as secondary sources from experts in the field, people involved in the cases, legal analysts, and other commentators opining on the implications and legacy of the chosen cases. An annotated table of contents, an in-depth introduction, and prefaces that overview each case all provide context as readers delve into the topic at hand. To help students fully probe the subject, each volume contains book and periodical bibliographies, a comprehensive index, and a list of organizations to contact. With these features, the Issues on Trial series offers a well-rounded perspective on the courts' role in framing society's thorniest, most impassioned debates.

Introduction

Very few people would make an argument that political corruption is good or that there should not be ways of investigating and prosecuting dishonest politicians; however, attempts to eliminate corruption often conflict with other things that are valued in government. The act of holding officials and representatives accountable, for example, can interfere with the separation of powers between the executive, legislative, and judicial branches. In addition, limiting the impact that money has on political campaigns by controlling spending on advertising raises concerns about government interference with free speech. When laws for fighting corruption clash with other political values, they have frequently come under review by the judicial branch, including the Supreme Court.

An example of such a clash of fundamental values is the battle over "executive privilege." Though the term was coined in the 1950s by President Dwight Eisenhower, the concept that the president has the right to conceal information from exposure to Congress or the public goes back to the beginning of the republic. George Washington reasoned that the president needs absolute secrecy in some situations, such as the negotiation of a treaty with a foreign government. President Eisenhower argued that executive privilege was necessary because presidential advisers must be able to give full and frank advice to their boss in complete confidence. Eisenhower felt so strongly about this, he declared in 1954 that "any man who testifies to Congress about what advice he gave me will not be working for me by nightfall."

President Richard Nixon invoked the need for confidential discussions within the executive branch during the Watergate scandal of the early seventies, probably the most famous case of political corruption in the history of the United States. Named after the Washington, D.C., hotel where the Democratic National Committee (DNC) headquarters was located, the Watergate affair centered on the cover-up of a failed attempt to place electronic listening devices ("bugs") in the DNC offices during the 1972 presidential election campaign. In June of that year, two men were arrested in connection with a break-in at the hotel, and the Federal Bureau of Investigation determined that their activities were connected with the Nixon reelection effort. In May of 1973 the Senate launched hearings to determine whether the Nixon White House was directly involved in the crime. A special prosecutor, Archibald Cox, was appointed to head an investigation.

Having learned that the White House recorded all conversations and telephone calls in the Oval Office, congressional investigators and Cox attempted to obtain the tapes. In the fall of 1973, Cox was fired by Nixon, but Nixon was forced to appoint another special prosecutor, Leon Jaworski. The president held firm in his decision not to turn over the tapes. He did not comply in full with either court subpoenas resulting from Jaworski's investigation or with congressional subpoenas. By the summer of 1974, there were still sixty-four recorded conversations that Nixon refused to release. Having fought disclosure of the tapes all the way to the Supreme Court, on July 8, 1974, his attorneys argued before the justices that executive privilege protected the president from having to release the recordings to Jaworski's investigators. Sixteen days later the Court delivered a unanimous opinion rejecting the claim of executive privilege and ordering that the tapes be handed over to the special prosecutor. On July 27 the House voted in favor of the first article of impeachment (removal from office) against the president. Nixon, knowing that his defense would be irreparably hurt by information contained on the tapes, turned over the tapes and on August 8, 1974, resigned to avoid an impeachment proceeding.

The ruling in the case (*United States v. Nixon*) reinforced the important constitutional principle that the executive branch is subject to judicial investigation of its activities. The Court recognized that the presidency often requires confidentiality to carry out its functions effectively, as chief executives dating back to George Washington had maintained; however, to avoid corrupt or unconstitutional activities, the White House must be subject to judicial review. There could be no blanket granting of confidentiality, and if a prosecutor or other agent of the court had specific information indicating that documents or recordings were material to a case, the president would have to release the material.

President Nixon's attempt to use executive privilege to cover up corrupt activities illustrates the ways in which important political values can come into conflict with each other. Efficiency and effectiveness in government are generally desired, and the need for secrecy in many situations is widely recognized. The long tradition of chief executives claiming executive privilege—it was invoked as recently as 2007 by President George W. Bush—will no doubt continue. The doctrine can even be considered part of the "separation of powers" enshrined in the Constitution; confidentiality among executive branch officials can be used as a shield against abuse of power by another branch of the government. Indeed, Eisenhower invoked executive privilege during Senator Joseph McCarthy's Communist witch-hunt of the 1950s—events which most observers consider an abuse of congressional authority. Yet as the Supreme Court ruled in *United States v. Nixon*, the president's actions must be subject to legitimate investigation—particularly by the courts. Otherwise, executive branch officials could engage in corrupt activities with virtual impunity. Given the high stakes, it is likely that presidents will turn to the doctrine of privilege in the future, which may lead to additional Supreme Court cases addressing the concept.

The trade-off between the effectiveness of government and the ability to guard against corruption is just one example of how different goals in government can lead to legal conflicts.

Another instance is the desire to lessen the influence of large financial contributions in political campaigns. In today's politics, a large amount of cash is necessary to run a campaign, particularly to buy mass media advertising to get the candidate's message out. Several attempts have been made to combat the importance of big donors who supply the cash for such advertising. The most recent is the Bipartisan Campaign Reform Act (BCRA), also called the McCain-Feingold Act, enacted in March 2002.

Some big donors are groups, not individuals. In the past, substantial donations from groups such as corporations, labor unions, professional associations, or activist organizations could be given to political parties, earmarked for specific candidates. McCain-Feingold stopped this so-called soft-money stream. More controversially, the BCRA put restrictions on radio and television ads paid for by third-party organizations like those listed above, if the ads could be construed as supporting specific political candidates. These advertisements, also called "electioneering communications" were banned for a thirty-day period before primary elections and a sixty-day period before general elections. As the law was applied, any third-party ads mentioning candidates were banned. (The BCRA did *not* bar candidates from advertising with their own campaign funds.)

Opponents of the measure, led by Senator Mitch McConnell of Kentucky, charged that the law was an unconstitutional violation of free speech. In modern times, opponents of BCRA argued, political speech requires the use of mass media to be effective; limits on campaign advertising are contrary to the spirit and letter of the First Amendment. Another opponent, the influential conservative columnist George Will, called McCain-Feingold "the incumbent protection act," reasoning that

> by restricting the quantity and regulating the content and timing of political speech, the law serves incumbents, who

are better known than most challengers, more able to raise
money and uniquely able to use aspects of their offices ...
for self-promotion.

Supporters countered that the law's limits on television
and radio ads would cut down on negative campaigning and
help control the costs of attaining political office. By controlling these costs, the malevolent influence of money would be
lessened, the argument ran. The Supreme Court agreed with
supporters of the BCRA. In *McConnell v. Federal Election
Commission (FEC)* (2003), the Court held most of the law
constitutional.

Since the *McConnell* decision, however, a further case, *Federal Election Commission v. Wisconsin Right to Life, Inc.* (2007),
has granted an exception to the BCRA's thirty- and sixty-day
limits. Now third-party, issue-oriented ads that do mention
candidates but do not explicitly support (or oppose) them
cannot be banned. For example, a Right to Life group could
run a radio advertisement urging listeners to contact a particular senator or representative in regard to a change in abor-
tion law.

It is evident from the two cases described above that the
struggle for an honest government is not a simple matter of
good guys versus bad guys. The battles over executive privilege
and campaign reform show that the fight against political corruption has been complicated by other aspects of effective
democratic government. These cases are not alone. The case
of *Morrison v. Olson* (1988) deals with issues of separation of
powers between Congress and the President. *Sabri v. United
States* (2004), which addresses how much the federal government can become involved in local corruption investigations,
brings up issues of the rights of states and municipalities under the federal system of decentralized power. These judicial
decisions, along with *United States v. Nixon* and *McConnell v.
FEC*, are examined in *Issues on Trial: Political Corruption*.

CHAPTER 1

Political Corruption and the Abuse of Executive Privilege

Case Overview

United States v. Nixon (1974)

The United States Constitution divides the federal government into three branches: legislative (the Congress), executive (the President), and judicial (federal courts, headed by the Supreme Court). The Framers were concerned about the power of government and sought, in the words of James Madison, to "let ambition counter ambition," setting up a system whereby the different parts of government would be somewhat in conflict. By doing this, the Framers sought to ensure that no one person or faction could gain complete control over the power of the government—a situation they saw as dangerous to individual liberty.

One of the side effects of this system is that each branch is somewhat suspicious of the other; the executive branch is especially wary of revealing too much about its operations to the legislature. From the beginning of the republic, presidents have attempted to conceal information from Congress. They have done so under the doctrine of executive privilege—the principle that conversations or memoranda between officials of the executive branch are confidential and do not have to be revealed to Congress or the judiciary. The defense of executive privilege is generally twofold: first, it is necessary if the presidency is to maintain fully separate powers from the Congress, and, second, national security will be threatened if the protection of executive privilege is weakened.

The separation of powers justification for executive privilege holds that the president and his or her advisers must be free to have open and frank discussions of political matters. At times these might be politically damaging if revealed to the public or to Congress. Without executive privilege protecting these conversations, the president's advisers might feel restrained in what they can say, and thus be prevented from offering full and frank advice.

Executive privilege is also often justified on national security grounds. Presidents have traditionally been reluctant to disclose information to Congress about the conduct of wars, intelligence operations, or details of treaty negotiations. They fear that leaks to the public could undermine defense policies or treaty negotiations. Even the first president, George Washington, refused to release details of the negotiations of a treaty with England; he argued that as only the Senate was required to ratify treaties, only the Senate should have the right to details of treaty negotiations.

Since Washington's time, the Congress, the presidency, and the judiciary have repeatedly come into conflict over executive privilege. The epitome of these struggles came during the Watergate scandal. During the election campaign of 1972, some of President Richard Nixon's aides were linked to a failed burglary at the Democratic headquarters in the Watergate Hotel. President Nixon sought to hide any evidence of White House involvement and moved to prevent his aides from presenting sworn testimony on the affair. He claimed that any conversations between presidential aides, either with each other or with the president, were covered under a broad definition of executive privilege. Neither Congress nor the courts could force the White House team to testify or produce documents.

The Supreme Court, ruling unanimously, disagreed, specifically on the right of executive privilege being used to prevent testimony. In his written opinion, Chief Justice Warren Burger noted that executive privilege had always been justified with reference to specific national security or separation of powers concerns. The president and his staff had no blanket right to executive privilege; such a right would make the oversight of the presidency by the courts and Congress impossible.

> "Nowhere in the Constitution ... is there any explicit reference to a privilege of confidentiality."

Majority Opinion: Executive Privilege Cannot Shield Wrongdoing

Warren Burger

Warren Burger was appointed chief justice of the Supreme Court in 1969 by President Richard Nixon, the man he ruled against in United States v. Nixon.

The Burger Court unanimously rejected Nixon's attempt to avoid turning audiotapes related to the Watergate burglary over to a federal court. Nixon claimed that separation of powers and a constitutional right to confidentiality within the executive branch gave him the privilege of not releasing the tapes. Burger, however, insisted that the president's powers—enumerated in Article II of the Constitution—cannot overrule the judiciary's Article III powers of overseeing the other branches of government. As for an executive privilege of confidentiality, protected communications must be connected with a vital interest such as national security. In this case, according to Burger, Nixon failed to show any such connection.

We turn to the claim [by Richard Nixon] that the subpoena should be quashed because it demands "confidential conversation between a President and his close advi-

Warren Burger, unanimous opinion, *United States v. Nixon*, U.S. Supreme Court, July 24, 1974.

sors that it would be inconsistent with the public interest to produce." The first contention is a broad claim that the separation of powers doctrine precludes judicial review of a President's claim of privilege. The second contention is that if he does not prevail on the claim of absolute privilege, the court should hold as a matter of constitutional law that the privilege prevails over the subpoena duces tecum [a summons to produce tangible evidence for a trial].

In the performance of assigned constitutional duties each branch of the Government must initially interpret the Constitution, and the interpretation of its powers by any branch is due great respect from the others. The President's counsel, as we have noted, reads the Constitution as providing an absolute privilege of confidentiality for all Presidential communications. Many decisions of this Court, however, have unequivocally reaffirmed the holding of *Marbury v. Madison*, (1803), that "[i]t is emphatically the province and duty of the judicial department to say what the law is."

The Court Has Final Word

No holding of the Court has defined the scope of judicial power specifically relating to the enforcement of a subpoena for confidential Presidential communications for use in a criminal prosecution, but other exercises of power by the Executive Branch and the Legislative Branch have been found invalid as in conflict with the Constitution. In a series of cases, the Court interpreted the explicit immunity conferred by express provisions of the Constitution on Members of the House and Senate by the Speech or Debate Clause. Since this Court has consistently exercised the power to construe and delineate claims arising under express powers, it must follow that the Court has authority to interpret claims with respect to powers alleged to derive from enumerated powers.

Our system of government "requires that federal courts on occasion interpret the Constitution in a manner at variance with the construction given the document by another branch." The Court [has] stated:

> Deciding whether a matter has in any measure been committed by the Constitution to another branch of government, or whether the action of that branch exceeds whatever authority has been committed, is itself a delicate exercise in constitutional interpretation, and is a responsibility of this Court as ultimate interpreter of the Constitution.

Notwithstanding the deference each branch must accord the others, the "judicial Power of the United States" vested in the federal courts by Article III.1 of the Constitution can no more be shared with the Executive Branch than the Chief Executive, for example, can share with the Judiciary the veto power, or the Congress share with the Judiciary the power to override a Presidential veto. Any other conclusion would be contrary to the basic concept of separation of powers and the checks and balances that flow from the scheme of a tripartite government. We therefore reaffirm that it is the province and duty of this Court "to say what the law is" with respect to the claim of privilege presented in this case.

Grounds for Absolute Privilege

In support of his claim of absolute privilege, the President's counsel urges two grounds, one of which is common to all governments and one of which is peculiar to our system of separation of powers. The first ground is the valid need for protection of communications between high Government officials and those who advise and assist them in the performance of their manifold duties; the importance of this confidentiality is too plain to require further discussion. Human experience teaches that those who expect public dissemination of their remarks may well temper candor with a concern for appearances and for their own interests to the detriment of the decisionmaking process. Whatever the nature of the privilege of confidentiality of Presidential communications in the exercise of Article II powers, the privilege can be said to derive from the supremacy of each branch within its own assigned area of constitutional duties. Certain powers and privileges flow from the nature of enumerated powers; the protection of the confidentiality of Presidential communications has similar constitutional underpinnings.

The second ground asserted by the President's counsel in support of the claim of absolute privilege rests on the doctrine of separation of powers. Here it is argued that the independence of the Executive Branch within its own sphere insulates a President from a judicial subpoena in an ongoing criminal prosecution, and thereby protects confidential Presidential communications.

Balancing Presidential Interests with Judicial Oversight

However, neither the doctrine of separation of powers, nor the need for confidentiality of high-level communications, without more, can sustain an absolute, unqualified Presidential privilege of immunity from judicial process under all circumstances. The President's need for complete candor and objectivity from advisers calls for great deference from the courts. However, when the privilege depends solely on the broad, undifferentiated claim of public interest in the confidentiality of such conversations, a confrontation with other values arises. Absent a claim of need to protect military, diplomatic, or sensitive national security secrets, we find it difficult to accept the argument that even the very important interest in confidentiality of Presidential communications is significantly diminished by production of such material for in camera [in private chambers] inspection with all the protection that a district court will be obliged to provide.

The impediment that an absolute, unqualified privilege would place in the way of the primary constitutional duty of the Judicial Branch to do justice in criminal prosecutions would plainly conflict with the function of the courts under Article III [of the Constitution]. In designing the structure of our Government and dividing and allocating the sovereign power among three co-equal branches, the Framers of the Constitution sought to provide a comprehensive system, but the separate powers were not intended to operate with absolute independence.

> While the Constitution diffuses power the better to secure liberty, it also contemplates that practice will integrate the dispersed powers into a workable government. It enjoins upon its branches separateness but interdependence, autonomy but reciprocity.

To read the Article II powers of the President as providing an absolute privilege as against a subpoena essential to enforcement of criminal statutes on no more than a generalized claim of the public interest in confidentiality of nonmilitary and nondiplomatic discussions would upset the constitutional balance of "a workable government" and gravely impair the role of the courts under Article III. . . .

The Rule of Law Is Paramount

In this case the President challenges a subpoena served on him as a third party requiring the production of materials for use in a criminal prosecution; he does so on the claim that he has a privilege against disclosure of confidential communications. He does not place his claim of privilege on the ground they are military or diplomatic secrets. As to these areas of Article II duties the courts have traditionally shown the utmost deference to Presidential responsibilities. In *C. & S. Air Lines v. Waterman S. S. Corp.* (1948), dealing with Presidential authority involving foreign policy considerations, the Court said:

The President, both as Commander-in-Chief and as the Nation's organ for foreign affairs, has available intelligence services whose reports are not and ought not to be published to the world. It would be intolerable that courts, without the relevant information, should review and perhaps nullify actions of the Executive taken on information properly held secret.

In *United States v. Reynolds* (1953), dealing with a claimant's demand for evidence in a Tort Claims Act case against the Government, the Court said:

It may be possible to satisfy the court, from all the circumstances of the case, that there is a reasonable danger that compulsion of the evidence will expose military matters which, in the interest of national security, should not be divulged. When this is the case, the occasion for the privilege is appropriate, and the court should not jeopardize the security which the privilege is meant to protect by insisting upon an examination of the evidence, even by the judge alone, in chambers.

No case of the Court, however, has extended this high degree of deference to a President's generalized interest in confidentiality. Nowhere in the Constitution, as we have noted earlier, is there any explicit reference to a privilege of confidentiality, yet to the extent this interest relates to the effective discharge of a President's powers, it is constitutionally based.

The right to the production of all evidence at a criminal trial similarly has constitutional dimensions. The Sixth Amendment explicitly confers upon every defendant in a criminal trial the right "to be confronted with the witnesses against him" and "to have compulsory process for obtaining witnesses in his favor." Moreover, the Fifth Amendment also guarantees that no person shall be deprived of liberty without due process of law. It is the manifest duty of the courts to vindicate those guarantees, and to accomplish that it is essential that all relevant and admissible evidence be produced.

Due Process Outweighs Privilege

In this case we must weigh the importance of the general privilege of confidentiality of Presidential communications in performance of the President's responsibilities against the inroads of such a privilege on the fair administration of criminal justice. The interest in preserving confidentiality is weighty indeed and entitled to great respect. However, we cannot conclude that advisers will be moved to temper the candor of their remarks by the infrequent occasions of disclosure because of the possibility that such conversations will be called for in the context of a criminal prosecution.

On the other hand, the allowance of the privilege to withhold evidence that is demonstrably relevant in a criminal trial would cut deeply into the guarantee of due process of law and gravely impair the basic function of the courts. A President's acknowledged need for confidentiality in the communications of his office is general in nature, whereas the constitutional need for production of relevant evidence in a criminal proceeding is specific and central to the fair adjudication of a particular criminal case in the administration of justice. Without access to specific facts a criminal prosecution may be totally frustrated. The President's broad interest in confidentiality of communications will not be vitiated by disclosure of a limited number of conversations preliminarily shown to have some bearing on the pending criminal cases.

We conclude that when the ground for asserting privilege as to subpoenaed materials sought for use in a criminal trial is based only on the generalized interest in confidentiality, it cannot prevail over the fundamental demands of due process of law in the fair administration of criminal justice. The generalized assertion of privilege must yield to the demonstrated, specific need for evidence in a pending criminal trial.

> "What is at stake ... is not simply a question of confidentiality but the integrity of the decision making process at the very highest levels of our Government."

Effective Government Requires That Cabinet Conversations Remain Confidential

Richard M. Nixon

Richard M. Nixon was a congressman, a vice president, and in 1960 a losing presidential candidate. He eventually won the presidency in 1968. Because of his involvement in the cover-up of a burglary of Democratic political offices in the Watergate Hotel in Washington, he was eventually forced to resign the presidency in 1974.

In this speech regarding his view of executive privilege, Nixon makes a distinction between cabinet officials—such as the secretary of defense—and his personal aides, such as the White House chief of staff. He directs cabinet officers to testify before Congress because they are public officials; however, he thinks that executive privilege shields personal advisers from the requirement to testify before the legislative branch. The president needs such advisers to be candid when discussing politics and policy; frank discussion within the executive sphere requires that the president's conversations with advisers be kept confidential, he maintains.

Richard M. Nixon, "Statement of the President [on Executive Privilege]," *The Weekly Compilation of Presidential Documents*, March 12, 1973 [available at www.watergateinfo .com].

During my press conference of January 31, 1973, I stated that I would issue a statement outlining my views on executive privilege.

The doctrine of executive privilege is well established. It was first invoked by President [George] Washington, and it has been recognized and utilized by our Presidents for almost 200 years since that time. The doctrine is rooted in the Constitution, which vests "the Executive Power" soley in the President, and it is designed to protect communication within the executive branch in a variety of circumstances in time of both war and peace. Without such protection, our military security, our relations with other countries, our law enforcement procedure, and many other aspects of the national interest could be significantly damaged and the decision making process of the executive branch could be impaired.

The general policy of this Administration regarding the use of executive privilege during the next 4 years will be the same as the one we have followed during the past 4 years and which I outlined in my press conference: Executive privilege will not be used as a shield to prevent embarrassing information from being made available but will be exercised only in those particular instances in which disclosure would harm the public interest.

Policy on Withholding Information

I first enunciated this policy in a memorandum of March 24, 1969, which I sent to Cabinet officers and heads of agencies. The memorandum read in part:

> The policy of this Administration is to comply to the fullest extent possible with Congressional requests for information. While the Executive branch has the responsibility of withholding certain information, the disclosure of which would be incompatible with the public interest, this Administration will invoke this authority only in the most compelling circumstances and after a rigorous inquiry into the actual need

for its exercise. For those reasons Executive privilege will not be used without specific Presidential approval.

In recent weeks, questions have been raised about the availability of officials in the executive branch to present testimony before committees of the Congress. As my 1969 memorandum dealt primarily with guidelines for providing information to the Congress and did not focus specifically on appearances by officers of the executive branch and members of the President's personal staff, it would be useful to outline my policies concerning the latter question.

During the first 4 years of my Presidency, hundreds of Administration officials spent thousands of hours freely testifying before committees of the Congress. Secretary of Defense [Melvin] Laird, for instance, made 86 separate appearances before Congressional committees, engaging in 397 hours of testimony. By contrast, there were only three occasions during the first term of my Administration when executive privilege was invoked anywhere in the executive branch in response to a Congressional request for information. These facts speak not of a closed Administration but of one that is pledged to openness and is proud to stand on its record.

Personal Staff and a Need for Candor

Requests for Congressional appearances by members of the President's personal staff present a different situation and raise different considerations. Such requests have been relatively infrequent through the years, and in past administrations they have been routinely declined. I have followed that same tradition in my Administration, and I intend to continue it during the remainder of my term.

Under the doctrine of separation of powers, the manner in which the President personally exercises his assigned executive powers is not subject to questioning by another branch of Government. If the President is not subject to such questioning, it is equally appropriate that members of his staff not be so questioned, for their roles are in effect an extension of the Presidency.

This tradition rests on more than Constitutional doctrine: It is also a practical necessity. To insure the effective discharge of the executive responsibility, a President must be able to place absolute confidence in the advice and assistance offered by the members of his staff. And in the performance of their duties for the President, those staff members must not be inhibited by the possibility that their advice and assistance will ever become a matter of public debate, either during their tenure in Government or at a later date. Otherwise, the candor with which advice is rendered and the quality of such assistance will inevitably be compromised and weakened. What is at stake, therefore, is not simply a question of confidentiality but the integrity of the decision making process at the very highest levels of our Government.

The considerations I have just outlined have been and must be recognized in other fields, in and out of government. A law clerk, for instance is not subject to interrogation about the factors or discussions that preceded a decision of the judge.

For these reasons, just as I shall not invoke executive privilege lightly, I shall also look to the Congress to continue this proper tradition in asking for executive branch testimony only from the officer properly constituted to provide the information sought, and only when the eliciting of such testimony will serve a genuine legislative purpose.

Guidelines for Invoking Privilege

As I stated in my press conference on January 31, the question of whether circumstances warrant the exercise of executive privilege should be determined on a case by case basis; In making such decisions, I shall rely on the following guidelines:

1. In the case of a department or agency, every official *shall* comply with a reasonable request for an appearance before the Congress, provided that the performance of the duties of his office will not be seriously impaired thereby. If the official believes that a Congressional request for a particular document or for testimony on a particular point raises a substantial question as to the need for invoking executive privilege, he shall comply with the procedures set forth in my memorandum of March 24, 1969. Thus, executive privilege will not be invoked until the compelling need for its exercise has been clearly demonstrated and the request has been approved first by the Attorney General and then by the President.

2. A Cabinet officer or any other Government official who also holds a position as a member of the President's personal staff shall comply with any reasonable request to testify in his non-White House capacity, provided that the performance of his duties will not be seriously impaired thereby. If the official believes that the request raises a substantial question as to the need for invoking executive privilege, he shall comply with the procedures set forth in my memorandum of March 24, 1969.

3. A member or former member of the President's personal staff normally shall follow the well-established precedent and decline a request for a formal appearance before a committee of the Congress. At the same time, it will continue to be my policy to provide all necessary and relevant information through informal contacts between my present staff and committees of the Congress in ways which preserve intact the Constitutional separation of the branches.

> "Even though U.S. v. Nixon was a defeat for Nixon and a victory for executive privilege, that doctrine has not yet recovered from Nixon's abuse of power."

President Nixon's Abuses Endangered the Legitimate Use of Executive Privilege

Mark J. Rozell

Mark J. Rozell is professor of public policy at George Mason University in Virginia. His works on the presidency include Power and Prudence: The Presidency of George H.W. Bush *(2004) and* Executive Privilege: Presidential Power, Secrecy, and Accountability *(2002), from which this excerpt is taken.*

Rozell makes the case in the following viewpoint that President Richard Nixon attempted to expand the concept of executive privilege far beyond its traditional meaning. The president, according to Nixon, has unlimited power of executive privilege, which cannot be interfered with by other branches of the government. Moreover, according to Rozell, Nixon argued that all executive branch officials were covered by the doctrine. Nixon's justification for these assertions were to protect the office of the president and maintain national security. Rozell, however, believes that Nixon used executive privilege to cover his wrongdoing. By his actions, the disgraced president damaged the legitimate privilege for future chief executives, Rozell maintains.

Mark J. Rozell, "Undermining a Constitutional Doctrine," in *Executive Privilege: Presidential Power, Secrecy, and Accountability*. Lawrence, KS: University Press of Kansas, 2002, pp. 55–71. Copyright © 2002 by the University Press of Kansas. All rights reserved. Reproduced by permission.

President Richard M. Nixon went beyond the traditional defenses of executive privilege. Although he claimed, like his predecessors, to have used executive privilege for the public good, his actions did not evidence public-interest motivations. He invoked executive privilege for purposes of political expediency and used that power as a vehicle to withhold embarrassing and incriminating information.

The Nixon era brought about a fundamental change in the way that executive privilege is perceived and exercised. Prior to Nixon, many presidents confidently asserted this authority, and the coordinate branches of government generally accepted the legitimacy of executive privilege. In the post-Watergate era, most presidents have been reluctant to assert executive privilege, and many members of Congress have characterized all exercises of executive branch secrecy as Nixonian attempts to conceal and deceive. Nixon's exercise of executive privilege has had a profound and lasting impact on the status of that constitutional power.

President Nixon offered the most far-reaching, comprehensive definition of executive privilege imaginable under our constitutional system. He argued that (1) the president has an unlimited power of executive privilege; (2) under the separation of powers system, no other branch of government can question the president's constitutional authority in this area; (3) executive privilege belongs to all executive branch officials; (4) he had to strongly assert executive privilege during the Watergate investigations to protect the office of the presidency, but not himself, and (5) any breach of the president's absolute power of executive privilege would threaten the national security.

Unlimited Executive Privilege

Nixon tried to make the case that there can be no limitations on the president's use of executive privilege, that only the president himself has the authority to limit the use of executive privilege. In *Senate Select Committee on Presidential Campaign Activities v. Nixon* (1973), the president's defenders adopted this absolute executive privilege claim in their statement that "such a privilege, inherent in the constitutional grant of executive power, is a matter of presidential judgement alone." In the brief in opposition to the special prosecutor's demand for White House tapes, Nixon's defenders maintained that

> the privilege is not confined to specific kinds of subject matter . . . nor to particular kinds of communications. Reason dictates a much broader concept, that the privilege extends to all of the executive power vested in the president by Article II [of the Constitution] and that it reaches any information that the president determines cannot be disclosed consistent with the public interest and the proper performance of his constitutional duties.

After leaving office, Nixon went so far as to argue that there are no limits on presidential power generally. Nixon most clearly presented that view in his televised interviews with journalist David Frost. When questioned on 19 May 1977 by Frost about the limits on presidential power, Nixon replied, "when the president does it, that means it is not illegal." Such a statement implies that there are no limits on presidential authority, including the power to withhold information; all that is required is presidential approval of an action. In a clear refutation of the more common constitutional view that no person is above the law, Nixon argued that presidential actions have higher standing than the law itself. . . .

The Separation of Powers

During his presidency, Nixon adopted the view that Congress and the courts lack the authority to question or contest claims of executive privilege. In Nixon's understanding of the separation of powers, the president stands supreme and may unilaterally determine the scope and limits of his own powers.

Nixon believed that whenever a dispute between the political branches over executive privilege occurs, the president's claim of privilege resolves the dispute. In a sense, this view of the president in the separation of powers system elevates his role to that of participant *and* referee in a political struggle, because even the judiciary cannot referee disputes over executive privilege. In a revealing quote, President Nixon stated during the Watergate controversy that "the manner in which the president exercises his assigned executive powers is not subject to questioning by another branch of the government."

In the president's brief in opposition to the special prosecutor's demand for White House tapes, Nixon's attorneys offered the following view:

> In the exercise of his discretion to claim executive privilege the president is answerable to the Nation but not to the courts. The courts, a co-equal but not a superior branch of government, are not free to probe the mental processes and the private confidences of the president and his advisers. To do so would be a clear violation of the constitutional separation of powers. Under that doctrine the judicial branch lacks power to compel the president to produce information that he has determined it is not in the public interest to disclose. . . .

Nixon not only argued that the president's actions to protect the national interest cannot be unlawful; he also said that the activities of members of the executive branch are exempt from normal legal limitations if conducted on the president's behalf. "If the President, for example, approves something, approves an action because of the national security or . . . because of a threat to internal peace and order of significant magnitude, then the President's decision in that instance is one that enables those who carry it out to carry it out without violating a law."

To Nixon, executive privilege was not a power possessed only by the president and selected White House insiders.

Rather, in his view, executive privilege could be invoked by the president on behalf of *all* executive branch officials. Just as the president's exercise of power could not be questioned by the other branches of government, the president's aides could not be questioned. Nixon maintained that "if the president is not subject to such questioning, it is equally inappropriate that members of his staff not [*sic*] be so questioned, for their roles are in effect an extension of the president." . . .

Protecting the Presidency and National Security

In refusing to disclose information to Congress and the judiciary during the Watergate investigations, Nixon argued that in no sense was he acting merely to protect himself. Instead, he insisted, he was obligated to protect the presidency from improper encroachments on its constitutional prerogatives. During a question-and-answer session at a 17 November 1973 conference of the Associated Press Managing Editors Association in Orlando, Florida, the president responded to a query about his view of executive privilege. Nixon asserted that he had waived executive privilege for himself and his staff "voluntarily," so as "to avoid a precedent that might destroy the principle of confidentiality for future presidents." The president then cited what he called the "Jefferson rule" of presidential refusal to disclose information to the courts and Congress to protect the powers of the presidency. Referring to the [Aaron] Burr conspiracy case [in which Thomas Jefferson refused to present a letter for subpoena], Nixon explained as follows:

> Now why did Jefferson do that? Jefferson didn't do that to protect Jefferson. He did that to protect the presidency. That is exactly what I will do in these cases. It isn't for the purpose of protecting the President; it is for the purpose of seeing that the presidency, where great decisions have to be made, and great decisions cannot be made unless there is

very free flow of conversation, and that means confidentiality, I have a responsibility to protect that presidency. . . .

Finally, President Nixon asserted traditional national security concerns as justification for his use of executive privilege during the Watergate scandal. He argued that without the protection of executive privilege, "our military security, our relations with other countries, our law enforcement procedures, and many other aspects of the national interest could be significantly damaged and the decisionmaking process of the executive branch could be impaired."

Once again, the president's brief in opposition to the special prosecutor's demand for information stated the argument in favor of executive privilege:

> Disclosure of information allegedly relevant to this inquiry would mean disclosure as well as [sic] other information of a highly confidential nature relating to a wide range of matters not related to this inquiry. Some of these matters deal with sensitive issues of national security. Others go to the exercise by the president of his constitutional duties on matters other than Watergate. . . .

Abuse of the Constitutional Doctrine

President Nixon's view of executive privilege lacks constitutional and historical validity. In the unanimous *U.S. v. Nixon* decision, the Supreme Court made it abundantly clear that executive privilege is not an unlimited, unfettered presidential power. The Court strongly rejected the argument that, under the separation of powers system, the president's exercise of power cannot be questioned by the coordinate branches of government. Indeed, the Court reaffirmed its own authority to determine what the law is and to challenge the presidential exercise of power. Nixon's claim that only the president can determine the scope and limits of his own constitutional authority was indefensible.

There is no doubt that, under appropriate circumstances, national security is a sound basis for defending executive privilege. For Nixon, the problem was that he used the national security argument to cover up White House wrongdoing. In a 21 March 1973 conversation among Nixon, [White House chief of staff H.R.] Haldeman, and [White House counsel John] Dean, the president proposed using national security concerns as a Watergate defense:

> *President*: What is the answer on this? How can you keep it out? I don't know. You can't keep it out if [Howard] Hunt talks. You see the point is irrelevant. It has gotten to this point . . .
>
> *Dean*: You might put it on a national security basis . . .
>
> *President*: With the bombing thing coming out and everything coming out, the whole thing was national security.
>
> *Dean*: I think we could get by on that . . .
>
> *President*: Bud [Krogh] should just say it was a question of national security, and I was not in a position to divulge it. Anyway let's don't go beyond that.

Nixon persisted in claiming that his actions had been motivated by national security—even after publication of the White House transcripts revealed the sham, and even after he was forced to resign the presidency. In his 1977 interview with David Frost, Nixon recited Abraham Lincoln's words as supportive of the view that normally unconstitutional actions become constitutional when undertaken by the president to preserve the nation. Frost protested that "there was no comparison was there between the situation you faced and the situation Lincoln faced?" Nixon did not back down. "This nation was torn apart in an ideological way by the war in Vietnam, as much as the Civil War tore apart the nation when Lincoln was president." Nixon insisted that his actions must "be understood in the context of the times. The nation was at war. Men were dying." Further, he argued, "keeping the peace at home and keeping support for the war was essential in order to get the enemy to negotiate." Hence, Nixon defended the infamous Huston Plan, which advocated infiltration of antiwar groups through wiretappings, burglaries, mail openings, and other techniques. He also defended FBI wiretaps of National Security Council staff members and White House wiretaps of news reporters on the basis of national security. Nixon told Dean that the wiretaps were legal and covered by the doctrine of executive privilege.

The facts make it unarguably clear that Nixon did not use executive privilege during the Watergate scandal to protect the presidency—he did so to protect himself. Like his predecessors, Nixon claimed that he had to exercise executive privilege for the public good, but his actions betrayed that claim. The major result of Nixon's use of executive privilege was to politically discredit a legitimate, necessary constitutional power of the presidency. Even though *U.S. v. Nixon* was a defeat for Nixon and a victory for executive privilege, that doctrine has not yet recovered from Nixon's abuse of power.

> *"Presidents have long claimed . . . that the constitutional principle of separation of powers implies that the Executive Branch has a privilege to resist certain encroachments by Congress and the judiciary."*

The Battle over Executive Privilege Is Rooted in American History

Michael C. Dorf

Michael C. Dorf is the Robert S. Stevens Professor of Law at Cornell University Law School. He is a graduate of Harvard College and Harvard Law School.

The history of executive privilege stretches back to the beginning of the United States, argues Dorf in the following viewpoint. The doctrine was first used by President George Washington in a dispute with Congress over whether he must turn over documents regarding the negotiation of a treaty. In a case similar to the Watergate trial and President Richard Nixon's claim of executive privilege, Thomas Jefferson resisted turning over a letter that had been subpoenaed by a court judging a criminal trial. The conflict between the presidents who want to maintain secrecy and Congress and the courts trying to obtain information continues today, notes Dorf, with the president and others in the executive branch often resisting calls to publish information on policy issues.

Michael C. Dorf, "A Brief History of Executive Privilege, from George Washington through Dick Cheney," *findlaw.com*, February 6, 2002. Copyright © 2002 FindLaw, a Thomson business. This Column Originally Appeared On FindLaw.com. Reproduced by permission.

In a letter dated January 30, 2002, Comptroller General David Walker, the head of the non-partisan Government Accounting Office [GAO], announced that he would sue Vice President [Dick] Cheney, in order to obtain information about the National Energy Policy Development Group that Cheney chaired [in 2001]. The unprecedented lawsuit was made necessary, Walker's statement argued, by Cheney's refusal to cooperate voluntarily.

Walker's letter states that President [George W.] Bush has not claimed an "executive privilege" in connection with the GAO's information requests. However, signs indicate that the Administration likely will assert such a privilege as the case proceeds. Certainly that is the tenor of public statements by the Vice President and the White House. The GAO is an arm of Congress and accordingly, the Administration contends, its efforts to uncover the inner workings of the Executive Branch violate the constitutional principle of separation of powers.

Although claims of executive privilege have been made since the administration of George Washington, the law remains remarkably unclear, partly because the relevant actors have usually tried to avoid a direct confrontation if possible. Thus, who prevails in the [Cheney] controversy may turn out to be less a matter of what the law is, than of who blinks first: Congress, the Administration, or the courts.

What Is Executive Privilege?

The Constitution nowhere expressly mentions executive privilege. Presidents have long claimed, however, that the constitutional principle of separation of powers implies that the Executive Branch has a privilege to resist certain encroachments by Congress and the judiciary, including some requests for information.

For example, in 1796, President Washington refused to comply with a request by the House of Representatives for documents relating to the negotiation of the then-recently adopted Jay Treaty with England. The Senate alone plays a role in the ratification of treaties, Washington reasoned, and therefore the House had no legitimate claim to the material. Accordingly, Washington provided the documents to the Senate but not the House.

Eleven years later, the issue of executive privilege arose in court. Counsel for Aaron Burr, on trial for treason, asked the court to issue a *subpoena duces tecum*—an order requiring the production of documents and other tangible items—against President Thomas Jefferson, who, it was thought, had in his possession a letter exonerating Burr.

After hearing several days of argument on the issue, Chief Justice John Marshall issued the order commanding Jefferson to produce the letter. Marshall observed that the Sixth Amendment right of an accused to compulsory process contains no exception for the President, nor could such an exception be found in the law of evidence. In response to the government's suggestion that disclosure of the letter would endanger public safety, Marshall concluded that, if true, this claim could furnish a reason for withholding it, but that the court, rather than the Executive Branch alone, was entitled to make the public safety determination after examining the letter.

Jefferson complied with Marshall's order. However, Jefferson continued to deny the authority of the court to issue it, insisting that his compliance was voluntary. And that pattern persists to the present. Thus, President [Bill] Clinton negotiated the terms under which he appeared before Independent Counsel Kenneth Starr's grand jury, rather than simply answering a subpoena directing him to appear.

Executive Privilege in *Nixon*

Presidents often assert executive privilege even if the information or documents sought are not matters of national security. They argue that some degree of confidentiality is necessary for the Executive Branch to function effectively. Key advisers will hesitate to speak frankly if they must worry that what they say will eventually become a matter of public record.

The Supreme Court considered this argument in the 1974 case of *United States v. Nixon*. A grand jury convened by Watergate special prosecutor Leon Jaworski issued a subpoena to President [Richard] Nixon requiring that he produce Oval Office tapes and various written records relevant to the criminal case against members of Nixon's Administration. Nixon resisted on grounds of executive privilege.

The Court recognized "the valid need for protection of communications between high Government officials and those who advise and assist them in the performance of their manifold duties." It noted that "[h]uman experience teaches that those who expect public dissemination of their remarks may well temper candor with a concern for appearances and for their own interests to the detriment of the decisionmaking process."

Nonetheless, the Justices concluded that the executive privilege is not absolute. Where the President asserts only a generalized need for confidentiality, the privilege must yield to the interests of the government and defendants in a criminal prosecution. Accordingly, the Court ordered President Nixon to divulge the tapes and records. Two weeks after the Court's decision, Nixon complied with the order. Four days after that, he resigned.

Can Cheney Invoke Executive Privilege?

The Comptroller General's plan to sue the Vice President raises a host of unresolved legal issues. As a threshold matter, there is a question whether the courts will permit a representative of Congress (here, the Comptroller General of the GAO) to invoke judicial process against the Executive. The courts often rely on the standing and political question doctrines to avoid adjudicating conflicts between the other branches.

Nor is it clear, even assuming the court chooses to hear the Comptroller General's case, that the *Vice* President can assert executive privilege. The Constitution vests the Executive Power in the President. So long as the President remains healthy, the Vice President has no constitutionally assigned executive function. As far as the Constitution is concerned, the Vice President's role is legislative in nature: to preside over and break ties in the Senate.

Furthermore, the Comptroller General has not, to this point, requested information about what was said to or by Vice President Cheney's National Energy Policy Development Group. Rather, the Comptroller General has thus far only asked for the names of participants in the Group's various meetings. It is not clear that executive privilege, even if it applies, extends beyond the content of discussions to cover the fact that they occurred at all. (By comparison, the attorney-client privilege generally covers the content of consultations with a lawyer, but not the fact that they occurred.)

Executive Privilege and Private Citizens

Finally, no case to this point holds that executive privilege applies to conversations between Executive officials and persons *outside the government*, such as corporate officers of Enron and other companies.

The closest the courts have come to extending the privilege to such discussions was in the 1993 decision of the U.S. Court of Appeals for the D.C. Circuit in *Association of American Physicians and Surgeons, Inc. v. Hillary Clinton*. That case raised the question whether the Federal Advisory Committee Act ("FACA") applied to the health-care-reform panel chaired by then-First Lady Hillary Clinton. And that question, in turn, depended on whether the First Lady is, or is not, an officer or employee of the government.

Under FACA, if a person who is not an officer or employee of the government is a member of a government group, then the group's proceedings must be open to the public. The health-care-reform panel had kept its proceedings private, so if the First Lady was not a government officer or employee, it had broken the law. Fortunately for the Clinton Administration, however, the court held that the First Lady is indeed an officer or employee of the government, and FACA thus did not apply.

The court strained the statutory language in order to reach this conclusion—but why? The answer is that a contrary result—to be precise, a finding that the statute's requirement of public meetings applied to the health-care-reform panel—would have raised a difficult constitutional question. And, under a well-established principle of legal interpretation, courts construe statutes in order to avoid difficult constitutional questions. The D.C. Circuit applied that principle in this case.

According to the D.C. Circuit, the difficult constitutional question was this: Does executive privilege extend to conversations between Executive officials and persons outside the government? If so, then FACA unconstitutionally violates that privilege by requiring those conversations to be disclosed. Had the court ruled that the First Lady was neither a government officer nor a government employee, it would have had to decide the difficult constitutional question—for FACA then would have required disclosure of deliberations between the (non-government) First Lady and the executive branch government officials on the commission.

Why Cheney May Prevail

The relevance of this complex case to Cheney's situation is straightforward: The D.C. Circuit thought that executive privilege *might* extend to conversations between executive officials and persons outside the government. And any appeal in the Comptroller General's case against Vice President Cheney would go to the D.C. Circuit (before possibly going to the U.S. Supreme Court).

Thus, a claim of privilege by the Vice President could succeed—particularly if GAO were to go beyond its current requests and seek not only the names of people with whom Cheney consulted, but also the content of deliberations. The D.C. Circuit's speculation as to the breadth of the executive privilege indicates that even if private industry representatives acted as members of the Energy Group, the Group's deliberations may still be privileged, and thus not subject to FACA disclosure.

Will we soon learn the answer to the question the D.C. Circuit left open and the other puzzles surrounding executive privilege? Probably not. If history is our guide, it seems more likely that at least one branch of the government will find a way to avoid deciding the question directly. [Editor's Note: In February 2002 *Walker v. Cheney* was dismissed by Bush appointee U.S. district court judge John D. Bates.]

"[George W. Bush administration] officials ... have repeatedly expressed irritation at the limitations imposed upon
them by post-Watergate reforms, particularly those dealing with the tension
between scrutiny and secrecy."

Watergate Era Reforms Have Been Eroded Since 9/11

Matt Welch

*Journalist Matt Welch's work has appeared in major newspapers
such as the* Los Angeles Times *and Canada's* National Post. *He
is currently editor in chief of* Reason *magazine.*

*After the Watergate scandal, the Congress—particularly
members elected in 1974—instituted laws to ensure government
transparency. One objective was to curb the use of executive
privilege to hide corruption. Despite the just-concluded Watergate scandal, however, these laws were opposed by the Gerald
Ford administration. Thirty years later some of the same officials
who had resisted reform in the 1970s worked to erode the Freedom of Information Act and other transparency laws. In the aftermath of the 9/11 terrorist attacks, these officials justified their
actions with the same reasoning Richard Nixon used: Secrecy is
required both for the preservation of the powers of the president
and for national security.*

In November 1974, a reform-hungry Capitol Hill gave the
newly sworn-in President Gerald Ford one of his first real
challenges. Congress had passed a significant expansion of

Matt Welch, "Watergate Blowback," *Reason*, vol. 36, August/September 2004, pp. 14–15.
Copyright © 2004 by Reason Foundation, 3415 S. Sepulveda Blvd., Suite 400, Los Angeles, CA 90034, www.reason.com. Reproduced by permission.

Ralph Nader's 1966 Freedom of Information Act (FOIA), aimed at prying open for public scrutiny the previously exempt areas of national security and law enforcement. When Ford was vice president to a commander-in-chief famous for his secrecy, paranoia, and abuse [Richard Nixon], he had supported the new sunshine amendments. But as chief executive, the interim president allowed himself to be talked into a veto by his intelligence directors and by his young chief and deputy chief of staff: Donald Rumsfeld and Dick Cheney [who later became the first secretary of defense and the vice president, respectively, of the George W. Bush administration].

"This was their first battle at Ford's White House" says Thomas Blanton, director of the National Security Archive (NSA), a nonprofit at George Washington University that has helped declassify more than 20,000 government documents. It was a battle the FOIA foes lost: Congress overrode Ford's veto.

Battling Government Transparency

Thirty years later, Rumsfeld and Cheney are again squaring off against the advocates of government transparency. At press time, the Bush White House had yet to release the photographs and videos of the vile prisoner abuse at Abu Ghraib [prisoner-of-war facility in Iraq]; it's also defending its expansions of state secrecy in several cases before the Supreme Court. Its efforts are affecting not just Congress's and the press's ability to cross-examine the executive branch but citizens' ability to scrutinize how our tax money is being spent—and the government's ability to act without restraint.

"This administration just has a very fundamental opposition to the disclosure of records about government operation," says Tom Fitton, president of the watchdog group Judicial Watch. (Motto: "Because no one is above the law!") "I think the administration's general view is they'd like to see the end to all disclosure laws. . . . Barring that, they're fighting within the confines of executive privilege and secrecy."

Judicial Watch, as you may recall from the 1990s, came into national prominence with a series of lawsuits to pry loose documents relating to "Filegate," "Chinagate," "E-Mailgate," and other [Bill] Clinton scandals. "We're conservative—we're suspicious of big government," Fitton says. "I'm not aware of government secrecy as a conservative principle."

But as has become increasingly manifest during the course of George W. Bush's term, secrecy certainly has become a *governing* principle. Example: From fiscal year 2001 to fiscal year 2003, according to the federal Information Security Oversight Office, the number of documents classified by the government increased from 8 million to 14 million; the number of documents declassified has plummeted from 100 million to 43 million.

Different Century, Same Faces

With many of the same themes and characters making headlines in 2004 as 30 years ago (down to the central muckraking role of investigative reporter Seymour Hersh, who helped expose both Abu Ghraib and the My Lai massacre [of Vietnamese civilians by U.S. soldiers in 1968], and who was targeted for possible federal prosecution in 1975 by none other than Dick Cheney), the temptation to make analogies to Richard Nixon has become irresistible—even among Supreme Court justices. (The Court weighed the Nixonian precedents when hearing arguments on whether executive privilege shielded Cheney's meetings with energy executives.) Nixon counsel turned Watergate whistleblower John Dean has a new bestseller out that cuts to the chase: It's called *Worse Than Watergate: The Secret Presidency of George W. Bush*.

Does the analogy hold up? It's hard to imagine, given the depths of the Nixon administration's petty vindictiveness and depravity. (As Dean himself notes, Nixon's Joint Chiefs of Staff planted a spy in his National Security Council, which would be hard to picture today.)

But perhaps a more useful way of looking at the comparison is to note that many current [Bush administration] officials, from the president to the attorney general to the Ford administration vets, have repeatedly expressed irritation at the limitations imposed upon them by post-Watergate reforms, particularly those dealing with the tension between scrutiny and secrecy.

"In 34 years," Cheney told [journalist] Cokie Roberts in January 2002 on ABC's *This Week*, "I have repeatedly seen an erosion of the powers and the ability of the president of the United States to do his job. . . . One of the things that I feel an obligation [to do], and I know the president does too, because we talked about it, is to pass on our offices in better shape than we found them to our successors. We are weaker today as an institution because of the unwise compromises that have been made over the last 30 to 35 years."

9/11 and Increased Security

The September 11 [2001] massacre gave the administration all the political legitimacy it needed to begin dismantling those shackles. In short order:

- On October 12, 2001, Attorney General John Ashcroft issued a guidance memo to all federal agencies advising them to deny FOIA requests if there was any "sound legal basis" for doing so and assuring them that the Justice Department would provide any support necessary.

- On November 1, 2001, just as his father's records were about to be released to the public, Bush signed Executive Order 13,233, reinterpreting the 1978 Presidential Records Act to give the White House and former presidents unlimited discretion to veto the declassification of presidential papers. "The main thing it has done is just put a huge amount of delay in the system" Blanton says. "In 2001, before he wrote that Executive Order, the [Ronald] Reagan Library, for example, took about a year and a half, between 14 and 18 months, to respond to a request for documentation. Today, it's 48 months."

- On November 25, 2002, Bush signed the Homeland Security Act, which created a FOIA exemption for even nonclassified documents pertaining to what was vaguely defined as "critical infrastructure."

- On many occasions since, the White House has sought to extend executive privilege into uncharted territory.

The problem, Judicial Watch's Fitton and the NSA's Blanton agree, is that the administration's national security justifications are frequently bogus. "I'm not talking about the blueprints to a nuclear weapon, or our national defense and secrets related to that," says Fitton. "We're talking about using those types of national security arguments to just cover up corruption and things that are politically inconvenient."

Blanton says documents that administrations fight tooth and nail to suppress—such as the Pentagon Papers [that revealed information about Vietnam War policy], or the infamous August 6, 2001, presidential daily briefing about Osama Bin Laden [that told of a planned terrorist attack on the United States], or the 56-year-old Air Force accident reports [of the 1948 crash of a B-29 bomber during a test flight] whose classification formed the legal basis for withholding information on national security grounds—typically contain little or no truly sensitive information. "The banality of the thing is what strikes you," he says.

Forgetting the Lessons of Watergate

Watergate taught millions of Americans about the dangers of government operating without sunshine [i.e., transparency]. But Bush administration officials, especially those who lived through the scandal, learned an altogether different lesson—that checks and balances can be distractions and hand-cuffs.

"Corruption thrives in secrecy," Fitton says. "And if a bureaucrat thinks that everything he does is never going to see the light of day, and a politician or a political appointee thinks the same, then you can bet that the temptation to do incorrect things will be greater.

> If the idea is that what they can do can be exposed by an intrepid reporter or an activist group, it does keep people in line. And we're not talking about the speeding violations that often pass for ethics enforcement here in Washington. We're talking about, for instance, lying to Congress about the costs of a huge entitlement program. We're talking about bribery for pardons by the president of the United States. . . . These aren't technical violations of ethics rules; this is hammer-in-the-head stuff, and anyone who doesn't understand that this is wrong, and the secrecy surrounding it is wrong, frankly shouldn't be trusted with the public's trust."

CHAPTER 2

The Independent Counsel as a Tool Against Corruption

Case Overview

Morrison v. Olson (1988)

In the aftermath of the Watergate scandal of the early 1970s, it seemed unwise to leave the job of investigating the president or his top advisers to employees of the executive branch—namely federal prosecutors. There was an obvious conflict of interest for a lawyer to be called upon to investigate his superiors. Therefore, the sweeping Ethics in Government Act of 1978 created the Office of the Independent Counsel. This arm of government would, if called upon by the attorney general, investigate abuses in the executive branch of government. The goal was to create an investigating official as independent of the White House as possible in order to ensure that the president was not able to cover up misbehavior in office.

While this solution seemed obvious, the scheme was a matter of constitutional debate. Investigating crimes was by tradition and logic a matter for the executive branch, whose duties are to enforce the laws. The new office was nominally under control of the president, in the sense that the independent counsel must be appointed or dismissed by the attorney general who served the president. However, opponents of the law believed that a call from Congress for an independent counsel to investigate allegations of executive wrongdoing would force the administration to appoint such a counsel due to the public uproar that would result from a refusal. This left the executive with little real power either to avoid appointing an independent counsel or being able to stop an investigation once under way; the Congress was virtually creating a new branch of government.

These objections were raised by Theodore Olson and his legal team in his case against Alexia Morrison, the independent counsel appointed to investigate him and other officials of the attorney general's office. Olson was suspected of offering misleading testimony to Congress during a March 1983 hearing into the Superfund hazardous waste cleanup program run by the Environmental Protection Agency. He was also accused of conspiring with others to impede the Superfund investigation.

Olson refused to comply with subpoenas from the independent counsel to turn over documents relating to his involvement in the matter. The district court ruled in favor of the special counsel and held Olson in contempt of court, but on appeal, the ruling was overturned on the grounds that the law creating the office of special counsel was unconstitutional. The Supreme Court agreed to review the case, thus setting up a chance for a decisive ruling on the legality of the independent counsel.

In its decision, the Court ruled that the independent counsel section of the Ethics in Government Act was constitutional. Because she was appointed and could be fired by the attorney general, the independent counsel was an "inferior" official. The so-called appointments clause of Article II of the Constitution gives the president the right to appoint, with the consent of the Senate, cabinet-level officials. However, it reserves for Congress the right to appoint "inferior" officials. Therefore Congress acted constitutionally in establishing the independent counsel. Despite its being upheld, however, the independent counsel law faced continuing criticism as eventually both Democratic and Republican administrations became subject to lengthy investigations. The last straw was, perhaps, the Bill Clinton–Monica Lewinski sex scandal of the late 1990s, which saw public opinion turn against the independent counsel's investigation of a popular president. The law was allowed to lapse in 1999, and the functions of the independent counsel are now carried out by the Office of Special Counsel within the attorney general's office.

> "We do not think it impermissible for
> Congress to vest the power to appoint
> independent counsel in a specially cre-
> ated federal court."

Majority Opinion: Congress Has the Right to Appoint Special Prosecutors to Investigate Corruption

William Rehnquist

*William Rehnquist was appointed to the Supreme Court in 1971
and was made chief justice in 1986. He occupied that position
until his death in 2005.*

*When an official of the Environmental Protection Agency in
the Ronald Reagan administration, Ted Olson, was put under
investigation by a special counsel, he claimed the law creating
such a counsel was unconstitutional. It interfered with the
president's right to appoint top government officials and, more
generally, violated the principle of separation of powers. The Supreme Court disagreed, noting that both Congress and the judiciary had the constitutional right to appoint "inferior"
(noncabinet-level) officials who were subject to presidential control. The special counsel was just such an inferior official, said
the Court, because he or she was subject to dismissal by the attorney general.*

This case presents us with a challenge to the independent
counsel provisions of the Ethics in Government Act of
1978 [which prohibited the executive branch from investigat-

William Rehnquist, majority opinion, *Morrison v. Olson*, U.S. Supreme Court, June 29,
1988.

ing its own officials]. We hold today that these provisions of the Act do not violate the Appointments Clause of the Constitution, Article II, Section 2, Clause 2, or the limitations of Article III [on the judicial branch], nor do they impermissibly interfere with the President's authority under Article II in violation of the constitutional principle of separation of powers. . . .

Executive Appointments

The Appointments Clause of Article II reads as follows:

> [The President] shall nominate, and by and with the Advice and Consent of the Senate, shall appoint Ambassadors, other public Ministers and Consuls, Judges of the supreme Court, and all other Officers of the United States, whose Appointments are not herein otherwise provided for, and which shall be established by Law: but the Congress may by Law vest the Appointment of such inferior Officers, as they think proper, in the President alone, in the Courts of Law, or in the Heads of Departments. . . .

The initial question is, accordingly, whether appellant is an "inferior" or a "principal" officer. If she is the latter, as the Court of Appeals concluded, then the Act is in violation of the Appointments Clause.

The line between "inferior" and "principal" officers is one that is far from clear, and the Framers provided little guidance into where it should be drawn. We need not attempt here to decide exactly where the line falls between the two types of officers, because, in our view, appellant clearly falls on the "inferior officer" side of that line. Several factors lead to this conclusion.

First, appellant is subject to removal by a higher Executive Branch official. Although appellant may not be "subordinate" to the Attorney General (and the President) insofar as she possesses a degree of independent discretion to exercise the powers delegated to her under the Act, the fact that she can be removed by the Attorney General indicates that she is, to some degree, "inferior" in rank and authority. Second, appellant is empowered by the Act to perform only certain, limited duties. An independent counsel's role is restricted primarily to investigation and, if appropriate, prosecution for certain federal crimes. Admittedly, the Act delegates to appellant "full power and independent authority to exercise all investigative and prosecutorial functions and powers of the Department of Justice," but this grant of authority does not include any authority to formulate policy for the Government or the Executive Branch, nor does it give appellant any administrative duties outside of those necessary to operate her office. The Act specifically provides that, in policy matters, appellant is to comply to the extent possible with the policies of the Department.

Third, appellant's office is limited in jurisdiction. Not only is the Act itself restricted in applicability to certain federal officials suspected of certain serious federal crimes, but an independent counsel can only act within the scope of the jurisdiction that has been granted by the Special Division pursuant to a request by the Attorney General. Finally, appellant's office is limited in tenure. There is concededly no time limit on the appointment of a particular counsel. Nonetheless, the office of independent counsel is "temporary" in the sense that an independent counsel is appointed essentially to accomplish a single task, and when that task is over, the office is terminated, either by the counsel herself or by action of the Special Division. Unlike other prosecutors, appellant has no ongoing responsibilities that extend beyond the accomplishment of the mission that she was appointed for and authorized by the Special Division to undertake. In our view, these factors relating to the "ideas of tenure, duration . . . and duties" of the independent counsel, . . . are sufficient to establish that appellant is an "inferior" officer in the constitutional sense. . . .

Congress May Appoint Executive Branch Officials

This does not, however, end our inquiry under the Appointments Clause. Appellees argue that, even if appellant is an "inferior" officer, the Clause does not empower Congress to place the power to appoint such an officer outside the Executive Branch. They contend that the Clause does not contemplate congressional authorization of "interbranch appointments," in which an officer of one branch is appointed by officers of another branch. The relevant language of the Appointments Clause is worth repeating. It reads:

> ... but the Congress may by Law vest the Appointment of such inferior Officers, as they think proper, in the President alone, in the courts of Law, or in the Heads of Departments.

On its face, the language of this "excepting clause" admits of no limitation on interbranch appointments. Indeed, the inclusion of "as they think proper" seems clearly to give Congress significant discretion to determine whether it is "proper" to vest the appointment of, for example, executive officials in the "courts of Law." ...

We do not mean to say that Congress' power to provide for interbranch appointments of "inferior officers" is unlimited. In addition to separation of powers concerns, which would arise if such provisions for appointment had the potential to impair the constitutional functions assigned to one of the branches, *Siebold*[1] itself suggested that Congress' decision to vest the appointment power in the courts would be improper if there was some "incongruity" between the functions normally performed by the courts and the performance of their duty to appoint. In this case, however, we do not think it impermissible for Congress to vest the power to appoint inde-

---

1. In *Ex parte Siebold* (1880), the Supreme Court upheld the right of federal officials to both investigate (an executive function) and adjudicate (a judicial function) election laws.

pendent counsel in a specialty created federal court. We thus disagree with the Court of Appeals' conclusion that there is an inherent incongruity about a court having the power to appoint prosecutorial officers. . . .

Delegation to the Courts

Appellees next contend that the powers vested in the Special Division by the Act conflict with Article III of the Constitution. We have long recognized that by the express provision of Article III, the judicial power of the United States is limited to "Cases" and "Controversies." As a general rule, we have broadly stated that "executive or administrative duties of a nonjudicial nature may not be imposed on judges holding office under Article III of the Constitution." The purpose of this limitation is to help ensure the independence of the Judicial Branch and to prevent the judiciary from encroaching into areas reserved for the other branches. With this in mind, we address in turn the various duties given to the Special Division by the Act.

Most importantly, the Act vests in the Special Division the power to choose who will serve as independent counsel and the power to define his or her jurisdiction. Clearly, once it is accepted that the Appointments Clause gives Congress the power to vest the appointment of officials such as the independent counsel in the "courts of Law," there can be no Article III objection to the Special Division's exercise of that power, as the power itself derives from the Appointments Clause, a source of authority for judicial action that is independent of Article III. Appellees contend, however, that the Division's Appointments Clause powers do not encompass the power to define the independent counsel's jurisdiction. We disagree. In our view, Congress' power under the Clause to vest the "Appointment" of inferior officers in the courts may, in certain circumstances, allow Congress to give the courts some discretion in defining the nature and scope of the appointed official's authority. . . .

No Threat to Judiciary

Nor do we believe, as appellees contend, that the Special Division's exercise of the various powers specifically granted to it under the Act poses any threat to the "impartial and independent federal adjudication of claims within the judicial power of the United States." We reach this conclusion for two reasons. First, the Act as it currently stands gives the Special Division itself no power to review any of the actions of the independent counsel or any of the actions of the Attorney General with regard to the counsel. Accordingly, there is no risk of partisan or biased adjudication of claims regarding the independent counsel by that court. Second, the Act prevents members of the Special Division from participating in

> *any* judicial proceeding concerning a matter which involves such independent counsel while such independent counsel is serving in that office or which involves the exercise of such independent counsel's official duties, regardless of whether such independent counsel is still serving in that office.

We think both the special court and its judges are sufficiently isolated by these statutory provisions from the review of the activities of the independent counsel so as to avoid any taint of the independence of the judiciary such as would render the Act invalid under Article III.

We emphasize, nevertheless, that the Special Division has *no* authority to take any action or undertake any duties that are not specifically authorized by the Act. The gradual expansion of the authority of the Special Division might, in another context, be a bureaucratic success story, but it would be one that would have serious constitutional ramifications. The record in other cases involving independent counsel indicate that the Special Division has at times given advisory opinions or issued orders that are not directly authorized by the Act. Two examples of this were cited by the Court of Appeals, which noted that the Special Division issued "orders" that ostensibly exempted the independent counsel from conflict of interest laws. In another case, the Division reportedly ordered that a counsel postpone an investigation into certain allegations until the completion of related state criminal proceedings. The propriety of the Special Division's actions in these instances is not before us as such, but we nonetheless think it appropriate to point out not only that there is no authorization for such actions in the Act itself, but that the Division's exercise of unauthorized powers risks the transgression of the constitutional limitations of Article III that we have just discussed.

Separation of Powers Objections

We now turn to consider whether the Act is invalid under the constitutional principle of separation of powers. Two related issues must be addressed: the first is whether the provision of the Act restricting the Attorney General's power to remove the independent counsel to only those instances in which he can show "good cause," taken by itself, impermissibly interferes with the President's exercise of his constitutionally appointed functions. The second is whether, taken as a whole, the Act violates the separation of powers by reducing the President's ability to control the prosecutorial powers wielded by the independent counsel. . . .

This case does not involve an attempt by Congress itself to gain a role in the removal of executive officials other than its established powers of impeachment and conviction. The Act instead puts the removal power squarely in the hands of the Executive Branch; an independent counsel may be removed from office, "only by the personal action of the Attorney General, and only for good cause." There is no requirement of congressional approval of the Attorney General's removal decision, though the decision is subject to judicial review. . . .

Considering for the moment the "good cause" removal provision in isolation from the other parts of the Act at issue in this case, we cannot say that the imposition of a "good cause" standard for removal [of the independent counsel by the executive branch] by itself unduly trammels on executive authority. There is no real dispute that the functions performed by the independent counsel are "executive" in the sense that they are law enforcement functions that typically have been undertaken by officials within the Executive Branch. As we noted above, however, the independent counsel is an inferior officer under the Appointments Clause, with limited jurisdiction and tenure and lacking policymaking or significant administrative authority. Although the counsel exercises no small amount of discretion and judgment in deciding how to carry out his or her duties under the Act, we simply do not see how the President's need to control the exercise of that discretion is so central to the functioning of the Executive Branch as to require as a matter of constitutional law that the counsel be terminable at will by the President. . . .

No Significant Interference

The final question to be addressed is whether the Act, taken as a whole, violates the principle of separation of powers by unduly interfering with the role of the Executive Branch. Time and again we have reaffirmed the importance in our constitutional scheme of the separation of governmental powers into the three coordinate branches. . . . The system of separated powers and checks and balances established in the Constitution was regarded by the Framers as "a self-executing safeguard against the encroachment or aggrandizement of one branch at the expense of the other."

We have not hesitated to invalidate provisions of law which violate this principle. On the other hand, we have never held that the Constitution requires that the three Branches of Government "operate with absolute independence." In the often-quoted words of Justice [Robert H.] Jackson:

While the Constitution diffuses power the better to secure liberty, it also contemplates that practice will integrate the dispersed powers into a workable government. It enjoins upon its branches separateness but interdependence, autonomy but reciprocity.

We observe first that this case does not involve an attempt by Congress to increase its own powers at the expense of the Executive Branch. Unlike some of our previous cases, ... this case simply does not pose a "dange[r] of congressional usurpation of Executive Branch functions." Indeed, with the exception of the power of impeachment—which applies to all officers of the United States—Congress retained for itself no powers of control or supervision over an independent counsel. The Act does empower certain Members of Congress to request the Attorney General to apply for the appointment of an independent counsel, but the Attorney General has no duty to comply with the request, although he must respond within a certain time limit. Other than that, Congress' role under the Act is limited to receiving reports or other information and oversight of the independent counsel's activities, functions that we have recognized generally as being incidental to the legislative function of Congress. . . .

In sum, we conclude today that it does not violate the Appointments Clause for Congress to vest the appointment of independent counsel in the Special Division; that the powers exercised by the Special Division under the Act do not violate Article III; and that the Act does not violate the separation of powers principle by impermissibly interfering with the functions of the Executive Branch. The decision of the Court of Appeals is therefore *reversed*.

> *"If to describe this case is not to decide it, the concept of a government of separate and coordinate powers no longer has meaning."*

Dissenting Opinion: The Independent Counsel Law Violates the Principle of Separation of Powers

Antonin Scalia

Antonin Scalia was born in New Jersey and educated at Harvard Law School. He was appointed to the Supreme Court by president Ronald Reagan in 1986.

In this viewpoint Scalia attacks what he calls the technicalities that the majority stressed in upholding the special counsel law. Separation of powers is the heart of the Constitution, according to Scalia, and he quotes many of its framers to support his case that they gave each branch of government complete power within its own sphere. This enabled each branch to fight off the encroachment of the other branches. According to Scalia, this design ensures that no one branch will grow too powerful, a condition that helps protect liberty and democracy. Investigation is an executive function, so the executive must investigate corruption in its own ranks. This may seem like a conflict of interest, but past scandals have shown that the public and Congress can force the president to investigate his own office effectively.

Antonin Scalia, dissenting opinion, *Morrison v. Olson*, U.S. Supreme Court, June 29, 1988.

The principle of separation of powers is expressed in our Constitution in the first section of each of the first three Articles. Article I, Section 1, provides that

> [a]ll legislative Powers herein granted shall be vested in a Congress of the United States, which shall consist of a Senate and House of Representatives.

Article III, 1, provides that

> [t]he judicial Power of the United States, shall be vested in one supreme Court, and in such inferior Courts as the Congress may from time to time ordain and establish.

And the provision at issue here, Art. II, Section 1, provides that "[t]he executive Power shall be vested in a President of the United States of America."

But just as the mere words of a Bill of Rights are not self-effectuating, the Framers recognized "[t]he insufficiency of a mere parchment delineation of the boundaries" to achieve the separation of powers. . . .

The founders conspicuously and very consciously declined to sap the Executive's strength in the same way they had weakened the Legislature: by dividing the executive power. Proposals to have multiple executives, or a council of advisers with separate authority, were rejected. Thus, while

> [a]ll legislative Powers herein granted shall be vested in a Congress of the United States, which shall consist of a Senate *and* House of Representatives, "[t]he executive Power shall be vested in *a President of the United States*." (emphasis added).

A Struggle over Power

That is what this suit is about. Power. The allocation of power among Congress, the President, and the courts in such fashion as to preserve the equilibrium the Constitution sought to establish—so that "a gradual concentration of the several powers in the same department" can effectively be resisted. Frequently an issue of this sort will come before the Court clad, so to speak, in sheep's clothing: the potential of the asserted principle to effect important change in the equilibrium of power is not immediately evident, and must be discerned by a careful and perceptive analysis. But this wolf comes as a wolf. . . .

[By] the application of this statute [the Ethics in Government Act] in the present case, Congress has effectively compelled a criminal investigation of a high-level appointee of the President in connection with his actions arising out of a bitter power dispute between the President and the Legislative Branch. Mr. [Theodore] Olson [an assistant attorney general] may or may not be guilty of a crime; we do not know. But we do know that the investigation of him has been commenced, not necessarily because the President or his authorized subordinates believe it is in the interest of the United States, in the sense that it warrants the diversion of resources from other efforts and is worth the cost in money and in possible damage to other governmental interests; and not even, leaving aside those normally considered factors, because the President or his authorized subordinates necessarily believe that an investigation is likely to unearth a violation worth prosecuting; but only because the Attorney General cannot affirm, as Congress demands, that there are *no reasonable grounds* to believe that further investigation is warranted. The decisions regarding the scope of that further investigation, its duration, and, finally, whether or not prosecution should ensue, are likewise beyond the control of the President and his subordinates.

If to describe this case is not to decide it, the concept of a government of separate and coordinate powers no longer has meaning. The Court devotes most of its attention to such relatively technical details as the Appointments Clause and the removal power, addressing briefly and only at the end of its opinion the separation of powers. As my prologue suggests, I think that has it backwards. Our opinions are full of the recognition that it is the principle of separation of powers, and the inseparable corollary that each department's "defense must ... be made commensurate to the danger of attack," which gives comprehensible content to the Appointments Clause, and determines the appropriate scope of the removal power. Thus, while I will subsequently discuss why our appointments and removal jurisprudence does not support today's holding, I begin with a consideration of the fountainhead of that jurisprudence, the separation and equilibration of powers. . . .

Exclusively the President's Power

To repeat, Article II, § 1, cl, 1, of the Constitution provides:

> The executive Power shall be vested in a President of the United States.

As I described at the outset of this opinion, this does not mean *some* of the executive power, but *all* of the executive power. It seems to me, therefore, that the decision of the Court of Appeals invalidating the present statute must be upheld on fundamental separation of powers principles if the following two questions are answered affirmatively: (1) Is the conduct of a criminal prosecution (and of an investigation to decide whether to prosecute) the exercise of purely executive power? (2) Does the statute deprive the President of the United States of exclusive control over the exercise of that power? Surprising to say, the Court appears to concede an affirmative answer to both questions, but seeks to avoid the inevitable conclusion that, since the statute vests some purely executive power in a person who is not the President of the United States, it is void.

The Court concedes that "[t]here is no real dispute that the functions performed by the independent counsel are 'executive,'" though it qualifies that concession by adding "in the sense that they are 'law enforcement' functions that typically have been undertaken by officials within the Executive Branch." The qualifier adds nothing but atmosphere. In what *other* sense can one identify "the executive Power" that is supposed to be vested in the President (unless it includes everything the Executive Branch is given to do) *except* by reference to what has always and everywhere—if conducted by government at all—been conducted never by the legislature, never by the courts, and always by the executive? There is no possible doubt that the independent counsel's functions fit this description. She is vested with the

> full power and independent authority to exercise all *investigative and prosecutorial* functions and powers of the Department of Justice [and] the Attorney General.

Governmental investigation and prosecution of crimes is a quintessentially executive function.

Depriving the President of Control

As for the second question, whether the statute before us deprives the President of exclusive control over that quintessentially executive activity: the Court does not, and could not possibly, assert that it does not. That is indeed the whole object of the statute. Instead, the Court points out that the President, through his Attorney General, has at least *some* control. That concession is alone enough to invalidate the statute, but I cannot refrain from pointing out that the Court greatly exaggerates the extent of that "some" Presidential control. "Most importan[t]" among these controls, the Court asserts, is the Attorney General's "power to remove the counsel for 'good cause.'" This is somewhat like referring to shackles as an effective means of locomotion. As we recognized in *Humphrey's Executor v. United States*,[1] (1935)—indeed, what *Humphrey's*

---

1. In *Humphrey's Executor*, the court ruled that President Franklin Roosevelt could not fire an official of the Federal Trade Commission (FTC). Scalia is arguing that it was not the "Good Cause" phrase in the FTC act that prevented the dismissal as the Court's majority argues, but that the FTC is a *legislative* agency.

Executor was all about—limiting removal power to "good cause" is an impediment to, not an effective grant of, Presidential control. We said that limitation was necessary with respect to members of the Federal Trade Commission, which we found to be "an agency of the legislative and judicial departments," and "wholly disconnected from the executive department," because

> it is quite evident that one who holds his office only during the pleasure of another cannot be depended upon to maintain an attitude of independence against the latter's will.

What we in *Humphrey's Executor* found to be a means of eliminating Presidential control, the Court today considers the "most importan[t]" means of assuring Presidential control. Congress, of course, operated under no such illusion when it enacted this statute, describing the "good cause" limitation as "protecting the independent counsel's ability to act independently of the President's direct control," since it permits removal only for "misconduct."

Independent Counsel Virtually Free of Executive Control

Moving on to the presumably "less important" controls that the President retains, the Court notes that no independent counsel may be appointed without a specific request from the Attorney General. As I have discussed above, the condition that renders such a request mandatory (inability to find "no reasonable grounds to believe" that further investigation is warranted) is so insubstantial that the Attorney General's discretion is severely confined. And once the referral is made, it is for the Special Division to determine the scope and duration of the investigation. And in any event, the limited power over referral is irrelevant to the question whether, *once appointed*, the independent counsel exercises executive power free from the President's control. Finally, the Court points out that the Act directs the independent counsel to abide by general Justice Department policy, except when not "possible." The exception alone shows this to be an empty promise. Even without that, however, one would be hard put to come up with many investigative or prosecutorial "policies" (other than those imposed by the Constitution or by Congress through law) that are absolute. Almost all investigative and prosecutorial decisions—including the ultimate decision whether, after a technical violation of the law has been found, prosecution is warranted—involve the balancing of innumerable legal and practical considerations. Indeed, even political considerations (in the nonpartisan sense) must be considered, as exemplified by the recent decision of an independent counsel to subpoena the former Ambassador of Canada, producing considerable tension in our relations with that country. Another preeminently political decision is whether getting a conviction in a particular case is worth the disclosure of national security information that would be necessary. The Justice Department and our intelligence agencies are often in disagreement on this point, and the Justice Department does not always win. The present Act even goes so far as specifically to take the resolution of that dispute away from the President and give it to the independent counsel. In sum, the balancing of various legal, practical, and political considerations, none of which is absolute, is the very essence of prosecutorial discretion. To take this away is to remove the core of the prosecutorial function, and not merely "some" Presidential control.

A Revolution in Constitutional Jurisprudence

As I have said, however, it is ultimately irrelevant *how much* the statute reduces Presidential control. The case is over when the Court acknowledges, as it must, that

> [i]t is undeniable that the Act reduces the amount of control or supervision that the Attorney General and, through

him, the President exercises over the investigation and prosecution of a certain class of alleged criminal activity.

It effects a revolution in our constitutional jurisprudence for the Court, once it has determined that (1) purely executive functions are at issue here, and (2) those functions have been given to a person whose actions are not fully within the supervision and control of the President, nonetheless to proceed further to sit in judgment of whether "the President's need to control the exercise of [the independent counsel's] discretion is *so central* to the functioning of the Executive Branch" as to require complete control, whether the conferral of his powers upon someone else "*sufficiently* deprives the President of control over the independent counsel to interfere impermissibly with [his] constitutional obligation to ensure the faithful execution of the laws," and whether "the Act give[s] the Executive Branch *sufficient* control over the independent counsel to ensure that the President is able to perform his constitutionally assigned duties." It is not for us to determine, and we have never presumed to determine, how much of the purely executive powers of government must be within the full control of the President. The Constitution prescribes that they *all* are. . . .

The Executive Can Investigate Itself

Is it unthinkable that the President should have such exclusive power, even when alleged crimes by him or his close associates are at issue? No more so than that Congress should have the exclusive power of legislation, even when what is at issue is its own exemption from the burdens of certain laws. No more so than that this Court should have the exclusive power to pronounce the final decision on justiciable cases and controversies, even those pertaining to the constitutionality of a statute reducing the salaries of the Justices. A system of separate and coordinate powers necessarily involves an acceptance of exclusive power that can theoretically be abused. As we reiterate this very day, "[i]t is a truism that constitutional protections have costs." While the separation of powers may prevent us from righting every wrong, it does so in order to ensure that we do not lose liberty. The checks against any branch's abuse of its exclusive powers are twofold: first, retaliation by one of the other branch's use of *its* exclusive powers: Congress, for example, can impeach the executive who willfully fails to enforce the laws; the executive can decline to prosecute under unconstitutional statutes, and the courts can dismiss malicious prosecutions. Second, and ultimately, there is the political check that the people will replace those in the political branches (the branches more "dangerous to the political rights of the Constitution") who are guilty of abuse. Political pressures produced special prosecutors—for Teapot Dome [conspiracy and bribery scandal] and for Watergate [Richard Nixon scandal], for example—long before this statute created the independent counsel.

> "Morrison ... *balances the interests of the executive branch with the demonstrated need to ensure accountability and respect in the eyes of the American public.*"

Separation of Powers Must Be Balanced with Protection Against Corruption

Kyriakos P. Marudas

Kyriakos P. Marudas is an attorney, sports agent, and film producer based in Baltimore, Maryland.

In the following article excerpt, Marudas praises the Supreme Court's decision in Morrison v. Olson. *He rejects what he calls the formalism of Justice Antonin Scalia's dissent, noting that much important legislation would be ruled unconstitutional by the judge's strict standard for separation of powers. Rather than a complete separation, Marudas believes that the powers conferred upon the president by Article II of the Constitution can be adjusted under limited conditions in order to further the accountability of the executive branch to Congress and the public. The* Morrison *decision, according to Marudas, will serve as a model for future separation of powers cases.*

Although it is undeniable that the independent counsel does reduce Presidential power, this diminution of executive power is quite proper. The rationale which underlies the Ethics In Government Act—that executive power be fully ac-

Kyriakos P. Marudas, "*Morrison v. Olson*: A Balanced Approach to the Separation of Powers Issue," *Maryland Journal of Contemporary Legal Issues*, vol. 1, no. 2, 1990, pp. 282–86. Reproduced by permission.

countable to the citizens of the United States—permits the independent counsel to pursue investigations of alleged violations of federal criminal law by executive officials.

One of the most eminent constitutionalists, James Madison, stated:

> In framing a government which is to be administered by men over men, the great difficulty lies in this: you must first enable the government to control the governed; and in the next place *oblige it to control itself.*

Thus, even if it were perfectly clear that the independent counsel prevented the President from fully accomplishing constitutionally assigned functions, an overriding need would nonetheless exist for such counsel in order to satisfy the paramount objective of executive accountability. What must take place is a balancing approach which factors the amount of power reduced in the executive branch with that of the amount of legitimacy and accountability gained for representative democracy.

One may argue that the executive branch can investigate transgressions of its own members, without recourse to an independent counsel. Conceding that this investigation can be done objectively (which may not necessarily be so), the fact that the executive branch is investigating its own people raises disturbing questions. As the Supreme Court explained [in its majority opinion in *Morrison v. Olson*], the appointment of a prosecutor interested in the outcome of the case, for reasons beyond the simple winning or losing, would "at a minimum create ... *opportunities* for conflicts to arise, and create ... at least the *appearance* of impropriety."

Formalism Fails

The formalistic method employed by Justice Scalia goes too far in abrogating the proper balance of power between Congress and the President. If any encroachment upon the executive's powers was improper, then many well-established Congressional acts would no longer be valid. For example, the

Freedom of Information Act enables citizens to have access to government documents, including those documents generated by the executive branch. If Scalia's line of reasoning is followed to its natural conclusion, the President's assertion of executive privilege would bar access to these documents because access would be considered an encroachment on executive power.

Furthermore, acceptance of Scalia's argument would endanger the procedures used by independent administrative agencies. One such agency that would be affected is the Federal Trade Commission (FTC), which is empowered under [Section] 5(b) of the Federal Trade Commission Act to investigate and prosecute individuals suspected of engaging in unfair methods of competition or unfair or deceptive trade practices. Under the Constitution, criminal law enforcement is assigned to the executive branch, which is obligated to ensure that the laws be faithfully executed. Thus, if Scalia's line of reasoning is followed, a challenge could be made that the FTC, in its criminal enforcement function, encroaches upon executive power.

Finally, one might argue that the effective way to voice displeasure over perceived unfairness in an executive investigation of executive officials is through the ballot box. Although this notion sounds workable in theory, it fails in practice. Citizens cast their votes for reasons that extend well beyond the handling of intrabranch investigations, encompassing such issues as the economy, foreign policy and the environment, to name a few. Therefore, it seems most unrealistic to view the ballot box as a credible deterrent to the misuse of executive power in executive branch investigations.

Role Carefully Limited

Given the parameters of freedom imposed on the independent counsel, it cannot be said that they impermissibly interfere with those powers accorded the executive branch. The independent counsel's role is limited to investigating certain federal crimes committed only by carefully enumerated government officials. Nowhere in the Ethics In Government Act or in *Morrison* is it indicated that independent counsel may establish federal policies or act as spokespersons for the government.

Essentially, Scalia's approach does not acknowledge that the powers conferred upon the President by Article II are capable of adjustment, so that the vital democratic tenet of accountability remains vibrant. Scalia utilizes a framework which has distinct boundaries separating the three branches of government, not recognizing the existence of interdependent spheres of activity among these branches. In contrast, Justice [Robert H.] Jackson stated the issue of separation of powers as follows: "While the Constitution diffuses power to better secure liberty, it also contemplates that practice will integrate the dispersed powers into a workable government. It enjoins upon its branches separateness but interdependence, autonomy but reciprocity."

The *Morrison* decision follows Jackson's flexible approach to the issue of separation of powers, striking a proper balance among the branches of our federal government. The decision recognizes that a strict separation of powers among these branches is not beneficial, especially when questions of accountability arise.

Unresolved Issues

The *Morrison* decision has significant ramifications for the constitutional status of independent prosecutors. By affirming the constitutionality of the independent prosecutors in an overwhelmingly favorable manner (7-1), it seems safe to conclude that future challenges to the constitutional validity of independent counsel are unlikely to prevail. Thus, *Morrison* can be viewed as deciding in a dispositive manner the constitutionality of the independent counsel provision of the Ethics In Government Act.

Nonetheless, a few items remain unresolved. Most promi-
nent among these items is the precise definition of inferior
and superior officers. It appears as if *Morrison* stands for the
proposition that the officer need not be "subordinate" in order
for that officer to be labeled an inferior officer. It is also apparent, however, that the officer must be under the authority
of a government official, to some extent. The extent to which
an officer's freedom of action is controlled by another is the
touchstone for determining whether the officer is inferior. Obviously, the greater the degree of control to which the officer
is subject, the greater probability that the officer will be
deemed inferior and vice-versa. Unfortunately, standards
which hinge on the extent of control are not susceptible to
uniform criteria. Rather, the determination of an officer's status must be made on a case-by-case basis.

A related issue which is not addressed adequately by the
Morrison decision centers on the "as they think proper" language of the Appointments Clause. This language vests Congress with considerable discretionary power to enable officials
other than the President to appoint federal officials of inferior
status. The Court in *Morrison* does not define the proper exercise of that power, other than by issuing a broad directive that
Congress not give the appointment power to an offical who
would be placed in an incongruous position. Presumably, the
appointment of independent counsels has as its rationale the
notion that Congress believed political accountability is pro-
moted best by having these counsel appointed by members of
the judiciary. Be that as it may, the Court's unwillingness to
address this issue is of concern, for as it now stands, Congress
may selectively decide who will appoint inferior officers, without the need to advance a justifiable reason for making the
particular selection.

A final issue which remains unclear is the exact scope of
an independent counsel's prosecutorial jurisdiction. *Morrison*
indicates that the Special Division has broad discretion to de-

fine the scope of the counsel's jurisdiction. However, no criteria are given by the *Morrison* Court that can serve as guidelines to the Division, apart from the admonition that the scope of jurisdiction must demonstrably relate to the facts of the given case. Consequently, the independent counsel provision is subject to future legal challenges that question the scope of an independent counsel's prosecutorial jurisdiction in individual cases. The basis of this challenge is that the Division, in defining the scope of jurisdiction, will have overstepped the bounds of the separation of powers principle. The issue of an independent counsel violating the separation of powers principle may resurface once more.

Model for Separation of Powers Cases

More broadly, *Morrison* signifies how judicial analysis of the separation of powers issue will be conducted. To determine whether a given branch's action impermissibly interferes with that of another branch, one would consider the degree of control remaining in the branch subject to a reduction of power. If sufficient control is retained by this branch, then no separation of powers conflict arises.

Further, *Morrison* indicates that the Supreme Court has adopted a functional analysis to the separation of powers issue, departing decisively from formalistic approaches. An example of this functional approach is demonstrated by the recent case of *Mistretta v. United States* [1989], where the Court dismissed the petitioner's claim that vesting the power of sentencing guidelines for federal crimes in the judicial branch violated the powers conferred to Congress. The Court held that Congress could properly delegate this power to the judiciary, and [in the *Mistretta* opinion] stated:

> In adopting this flexible understanding of separation of powers, we simply have recognized Madison's teaching that the greatest security against tyranny—the accumulation of excessive authority in a single branch—lies not in a her-

metic division between the Branches, but in a carefully crafted system of checked and balanced power within each Branch.

Morrison carves out a specific and limited exception to the prosecutorial functions of the executive branch, an exception which has support in historical precedent. In making this exception, the Court balances the interests of the executive branch with the demonstrated need to ensure accountability and respect in the eyes of the American public.

> *"The [Court's] approach [to separation*
> *of powers cases] takes into account both*
> *the formal limitations on the power of*
> *each branch and the ambiguity and*
> *overlap of powers that keep the system*
> *flexible."*

The Separation of Powers Doctrine Must Be Flexible

Katy J. Harriger

Katy J. Harriger is a professor at Wake Forest University, where she chairs the Political Science Department.

In this excerpt Harriger makes the case that Morrison v. Olson *was rightly decided. She criticizes legal "formalism" which, in its zeal to follow the letter of the Constitution, does not allow the flexibility necessary to resolve separation of powers disputes. The Court had been moving toward formalism, she asserts, starting with* INS v. Chadha *(1983)—in which the Court overruled a "legislative veto" that the Congress held over immigration courts—and continuing with* Bowsher v. Synar *(1986)—in which the Court struck down automatic spending cuts triggered by deficits found in budget reform legislation. Harriger contends, however, that* Morrison *marked a turning point for the Supreme Court in adopting a more flexible interpretation of the Constitution.*

Katy J. Harriger, "Is the Special Prosecutor Constitutional?" *Independent Justice: the Federal Special Prosecutor in American Politics.* Lawrence, KS: University Press of Kansas, 1992, pp. 111–15. Copyright © 1992 by the University Press of Kansas. All rights reserved. Reproduced by permission.

The Court's decision in *Morrison* [*v. Olson* (1988)] was an important one for two reasons, one having to do with its specific implications for the independent counsel process, the other having to do with its general meaning in analyzing the separation of powers. Its specific importance derives from its contribution to resolution of the constitutional uncertainty that had surrounded the independent counsel arrangement from its inception. In upholding the constitutionality of the provisions, it secured the ongoing investigations in the *Olson* and Iran-Contra[1] cases and the convictions in the *Deaver* [*v. Seymour*] and [*United States v.*] *Nofziger* cases [all cases handled by special counsels]. Moreover, the decision alters the balance in the debate over the continued existence of the provisions because it makes it more difficult for opponents to argue that the arrangement infringes to an unconstitutional extent upon the power of the executive. The fact that the opinion was authored by no less a conservative than William Rehnquist and had the support of seven justices gives great weight to the proponents' position. . . .

The Court's decision clearly rests on what it sees as the carefully constructed limits on the independent counsel and the court panel. Any attempts to alter those limits might open up the provisions to renewed attack. At this point, there is little incentive to do anything to the provisions, for as they stand they have the endorsement of a large majority on the Supreme Court.

More generally, *Morrison v. Olson* is important because it appears to signal a readjustment in the Court's separation of powers jurisprudence. After two decisions [in 1982 and 1986] that seemed to herald a new formalism in the analysis of separation of powers, *Morrison* and several cases that follow it suggest that the Court is unwilling to follow the formalist approach to its logical conclusion (or at least to the conclusion

1. The Iran-Contra scandal involved the Reagan administration's secret selling of weapons, despite federal law, to Iran in the 1980s.

that many conservatives hoped it would come to): that the theory of the unitary executive requires major restructuring of the modern administrative state. The Court's recent separation of powers decisions seem, on their face, to be inconsistent, for they rest on apparently contradictory "theories" of separation of powers, depending upon whether they are striking down legislative acts (rigid) or upholding them (flexible). . . .

Not a Revolutionary Decision

There is more sense to the Court's analysis of separation of powers questions than its critics imply. The Court's decisions rest on consideration of the textual and implied powers of each branch, its recognition of the particular political context surrounding each separation of powers case, and, perhaps, in its evaluation of its own powers and its historical role as referee in separation of powers disputes. When we consider these concerns as a whole, we see that *Morrison* was decided correctly and was not the "revolutionary" decision that [Justice Antonin] Scalia contends in his dissent. In fact, it has been suggested [by University of Virginia law professor Earl C. Dudley Jr.] that "adoption of Scalia's position at this point in our history was much more likely to revolutionize the conduct of government."

When reading the carefully controlled language of the majority's opinion in *Morrison*, it is difficult to take seriously Scalia's prediction that the Court has given Congress an open invitation to usurp executive powers. Rehnquist looks to the language of the text. He relies on the plain meaning of the appointments clause. He examines its history and usage. Having done all of this, he concludes that the appointment arrangement in the statute is not a violation of the clause. It is firmly rooted in the text of the Constitution and in the precedent interpreting that text. [Dean of the Chicago-Kent School of Law] Harold Krent argues convincingly that the formalist and functionalist debate over the Supreme Court's analysis of separation of powers misconceives that analysis and ignores the subtleties in it that give it an underlying logic. Krent suggests that the Court's decisions have at their base a "deceptively simple principle ... that the Constitution circumscribes the power of the branches by limiting the ways each can act." While the Constitution leaves the boundaries between the branches ambiguous, it clearly places limits on "how and when each branch can act." If we understand this to be the core of the separation of powers arrangement, then neither a rigid, mechanistic view nor a practical, flexible view is adequate to the task of analyzing the separation of powers in a meaningful way. Krent finds that the Supreme Court follows a two-step process in its analysis of disputes concerning the separation of powers. It asks whether the branches have acted within the constitutional limits placed on their actions. If they have, but a conflict between the branches is nonetheless unavoidable because of the overlapping of powers, then the Court asks what "is the best way to accommodate the overlapping powers of the branches?" In seeking such an accommodation, the Court balances the "potential for disruption" of one branch's powers with the justification or need of the other branch to act.

The Court and Separation of Powers

This approach takes into account both the formal limitations on the power of each branch and the ambiguity and overlap of powers that keep the system flexible and able to adapt to its world. The Court is taking an inherently sensible approach to separation of powers that is no more "inconsistent" than the Constitution itself. What remains to be considered, however, is what factors influence the way in which the Court strikes the balance when conflict between the branches is inescapable. It is at this point that the Court's recognition of the political realities of the case and its view of its own role in the separation of powers are likely to influence its analysis.

The background facts of separation of powers disputes are frequently charged with high-powered political ramifications. Deputy Independent Counsel Earl Dudley, Jr., argues that in the *Morrison* case there were two major political problems standing in the way of a Court decision against the independent counsel. The first problem was the implications of such a move for the validity of the "myriad arrangements of the administrative state." While a constitutional challenge to independent regulatory agencies had clearly been on the conservative agenda during the [Ronald] Reagan administration, a majority on the Court clearly was not willing to participate in the dismantling of an administrative arrangement that it had helped to legitimate. Striking down the independent counsel arrangement on the basis of the theory of the unitary executive would clearly have been a major step in that direction.

The other major political problem facing the Court was more directly related to the independent counsel. The immediate consequence of a decision to strike down the provisions would have been to make invalid two recently obtained convictions under the act, to dissolve the ongoing investigation of [assistant attorney general Ted] Olson that instigated the suit, and, perhaps most importantly, to call into question much of the work of the Iran-Contra independent counsel. . . .

Addressing Political Concerns

In cases concerning separation of powers it seems inevitable that the political facts should shape the outcome. The Court could not divorce itself from the pending constitutional crisis provoked by Watergate when it decided *United States v. Nixon*. The battle between [President Harry S.] Truman and Congress over the invocation of Taft-Hartley could not be ignored in the steel seizure case[2]. These political facts are woven into the

2. In *United States v. Nixon*, the Court ruled that President Richard Nixon had to turn over audiotapes to a criminal court, despite his claims of executive privilege. The Truman administration repeatedly clashed with Congress over Truman's refusal to use the Taft-Hartley Act, a law that severely restricted the actions of labor unions and that Truman had vetoed, to end various labor disputes.

fabric of separation of powers cases. They cannot be removed or ignored without altering the meaning of the case itself. The *Morrison* Court correctly took them into account in the case of the independent counsel.

Finally, some members of the Court may be influenced in their analysis of separation of powers by whether or not the judiciary is given a role in the disputed arrangement. In several of the Court's separation of powers decisions, including *Morrison*, the judiciary has been implicated in the dispute. When it is, the Court appears to be reminded of the value of a flexible approach to the separation of powers. Perhaps this lies in the value of knowing thyself and, thus, believing that ambiguous grants of power are not dangerous in the hands of the "least dangerous branch." This view may underlie the *Morrison* Court's willingness to accept duties that were not clearly "judicial" under the independent counsel arrangement, minimizing the threat that such an exercise of power might pose to individuals or the executive. . . .

Stepping Back from Formalism

The Court made the right decision in *Morrison* because it recognized the broader consequences of striking down the independent counsel arrangement. It was able to use the opinion to step back from the slippery slope of formalism down which it had appeared to be headed after [*INS v.*] *Chadha* and *Bowsher* [*v. Synar*]. Had it pursued this formalist approach in *Morrison* and adopted Scalia's view of the extent of executive power, it would have taken a major step toward finding independent regulatory agencies unconstitutional, a decision with enormous consequences for the modern administrative state and for the expansion of executive power.

> *"Under the statute many inquiries be-*
> *came political weapons even when they*
> *had mixed results in policing corrup-*
> *tion."*

Despite the *Morrison* Decision the Independent Counsel Law Has Lost Favor

Dan Carney

Dan Carney is an editorial writer at USA Today, *a national daily newspaper. He was a reporter at* Congressional Quarterly *from 1995 to 2000.*

Despite his loss in Morrison v. Olson, *which upheld the constitutionality of the independent counsel, Ted Olson had the last laugh, contends Carney in the following viewpoint. In 1999 the law expired, and few public figures in Washington, D.C., supported its renewal. The law had come under fire in the 1980s, with Republicans charging that it "criminalized politics" because many independent counsel investigations targeted Republican officials, Carney notes. The law actually expired in 1992 but was revived in 1994 by Congress and President Bill Clinton. Ironically, after the law's revival the Democratic officials in Clinton's administration, including the president himself, came under fire from several independent counsels. The independent counsel seemed out of control, Carney opines, perhaps confirming Justice Antonin Scalia's predictions about the independent counsel law. Both parties stood by as it expired for good in 1999.*

Dan Carney, "Who Polices Politicians After Counsel Law Expires?" *CQ Weekly*, June 26, 1999. Copyright © 1999. Republished with permission of CQ Weekly, conveyed through Copyright Clearance Center, Inc.

In December 1992, Theodore B. Olson, who had been an assistant attorney general in the [Ronald] Reagan administration, threw a party to celebrate the demise of the independent counsel law. But unfortunately for Olson, who was one of the earliest officials targeted under the law and remains one if its most vociferous critics, the festivities proved premature; the law was revised and reinstated a year-and-a-half later.

Now Olson has reason for another fete. The 1994 version of the independent counsel law lapse[d] on June 30 [1999]. "And this time," Olson says with considerable satisfaction, "I think it will stick."

Olson appears justified in his optimism, even in light of his previous disappointment. Unlike the last time—when reauthorization was quietly blocked by Senate Republicans just before Republican President George [H.W.] Bush stood for reelection—this time the opposition appears to be as bipartisan as it is vocal and widespread. Sentiment against the law has been fueled by the low standing in public opinion polls of the most famous independent counsel ever, Kenneth W. Starr; by the public's opposition to the impeachment of President [Bill] Clinton that grew from Starr's inquiry; and by the roster of exonerations, acquittals and mistrials that dominates the legal scorecard of cases brought during the 20 independent counsel investigations made public in the past 21 years. . . .

Some lawmakers and congressional experts see the demise of the independent counsel law as heralding a more civil era of political battle. Republicans and Democrats are not about to call a truce, they say, but may be signaling a willingness to unilaterally disarm themselves of a powerful weapon for settling their differences.

"It isn't that partisanship is going to be any less," said Representative Howard L. Berman of California, the ranking Democrat on the ethics committee and a member of the Judiciary Committee that turned Starr's findings on Clinton into four articles of impeachment [in 1998]. "It's just that we are trying to fence off certain areas." . . .

'Decriminalizing' Politics

Allowing the law to expire [may] help in the "decriminalization" of the political process, many of its opponents say, because under the statute many inquiries became political weapons even when they had mixed results in policing corruption.

"We have been so intent on writing detailed rules about political ethics, we have lost sight of what it means to actually have ethics," said Norman Ornstein, resident scholar at AEI [American Enterprise Institute]. "Now the system, I think, is finally adjusting, and trying to strike a better balance."

Even some lawmakers who want to revive the law say politics has become too much of a blood sport. "It seems like we have criminalized politics," [Senator Joe] Lieberman said in an interview June 11 [1999]. "And criminal investigations have become politics by another name. I just wish we didn't have to let the statute lapse to realize this."

Members of the public have been in front of lawmakers on the issue of independent counsels, registering their opposition in polls and a series of verdicts. A *Washington Post* poll of 1,010 people in February [1999], just after Clinton's impeachment trial acquittal, found 59 percent with an "unfavorable" view of Starr to 27 percent "favorable." . . .

One group that does not think these developments constitute a healthy trend is the Congressional Accountability Project, a non-profit group focused on making sure federal officials obey campaign finance and ethics laws. The group is concerned about letting the independent counsel statute lapse but is even more troubled by a change [in 1997] in House ethics rules, which now bar non-members from filing complaints with the ethics committee. The Government Accountability Project had used the old rules to force several inquiries by the Committee on Standards of Official Conduct. . . .

Few Convictions Have Resulted

Independent counsels were major distractions for Presidents [George H.W.] Bush and Ronald Reagan. And the Clinton presidency has been forever altered by Starr's probe.

But for all the prosecutorial power granted to independent counsels in the past two decades, their efforts have resulted in few lasting convictions of senior executive branch officials— even though the law was designed to enhance the scrutiny of those officials. Most of the lasting convictions have been of people who were subordinate or peripheral to—and whose malfeasance was tangential to—the stated targets of the independent counsels' efforts.

In 11 of the 15 investigations that have been formally concluded, no charges were filed at all. In three of those cases, the names of the onetime targets have been kept sealed. In another, Independent Counsel Joseph E. diGenova wrote a letter apologizing to the people he was called on to investigate.

At the same time, critics of the law say, dozens of secondary players have been prosecuted—and hundreds of innocent people have seen their lives turned upside down and their bank accounts emptied out—only because they had the misfortune of having some tangential connection to a line of inquiry being pursued by an independent counsel with officially unfettered curiosity. . . .

Return to the Past System

Before there was an independent counsel law, executive branch scandals generally were addressed by special prosecutors hired from outside the Justice Department and given objectives by the attorney general. This system [was] revived when the counsel law lapse[d], and Attorney General Janet Reno said June 24 [1999] that the Justice Department is working on guidelines—in consultation with Congress—for how she will appoint special prosecutors and oversee their work. . . .

What distinguishes the mood of 1999 from that of 1992 is that, by now, both Democrats and Republicans have been bloodied by independent counsels. Until Clinton's election, the statute had been written mostly by Democratic Congresses and used mostly against Republican administrations, in a type of a political corollary to Mark Twain's adage that "nothing so needs reforming as other people's habits."

But during the Clinton administration the Democrats' handiwork was turned against them, culminating in a presidential impeachment that grew out of Starr's scrutiny of a sexual affair that had not even begun when he was named to investigate a completely different matter.

"Democrats got a good object lesson in reality versus theory," said Berman. "We were all very imbued with the attractiveness of independent counsels. A lot of that came from Richard Nixon, and a lot of it came from 12 years of Republican rule. There was a theoretical attractiveness to the statute. But it met our partisan interests as well." . . .

Possible Solutions

[Political action group] Common Cause recommends handing allegations of executive branch malfeasance to the Justice Department's criminal division. The group would try to insulate the assistant attorney general in charge by making it more difficult for senior officials to overrule his or her decisions.

The commission assembled by AEI and Brookings [Institution] recommends an almost complete reversion to the old system. Decisions on whom to investigate and how to do so would be left to the attorney general under departmental guidelines on when a special prosecutor should be appointed. If a special prosecutor were appointed, the attorney general would be able to terminate the probe at the end of two years, or annually subsequent to that. At other times the prosecutor could be fired for good cause.

CHAPTER 3

Fighting Corruption by Limiting Campaign Spending and Contributions

Case Overview

McConnell v. Federal Election Commission (2003)

The Bipartisan Campaign Reform Act (BCRA) is the latest in a series of laws which have been designed "to purge national politics of what [is] conceived to be the pernicious influence of 'big money' campaign contributions," according to the Supreme Court. The BCRA (also called the McCain-Feingold law after its two main proponents in the Senate, John McCain and Russell Feingold) amended earlier attempts at reforming campaign finance, particularly the Federal Election Campaign Act (FECA) of 1971. While the legislation is multifaceted, one of its major goals is to close the so-called soft-money loophole, the ability of individuals and organizations to support candidates indirectly through donations to political parties or political activist organizations. According to proponents, the law was a necessary continuation of efforts to eliminate the influence of big donors on the political process. Opponents, however, consider the law's measures an attack on freedom of speech.

One of the later—and most controversial—features of the McCain-Feingold law was a limitation on campaign expenditures. For the first time, political parties and political action committees were restricted in how they could spend money they raised. While previous laws had limited individuals' and organizations' contributions to candidates, they were still able to give to parties and registered issue-oriented political committees. The parties and activist groups would then use the "soft money"—money not regulated by FECA—to sponsor television, newspaper, and other advertisements that would aid specific candidates. As long as such ads did not contain an explicit endorsement in a particular race such as "vote for John McCain" or "don't vote for Hillary Clinton," they were perfectly legal.

Labor unions, business lobby groups, and individuals were able to use this loophole to indirectly aid candidates; contributions to political parties could be targeted at specific electoral contests. Because the contributions to the parties were a matter of public record, it was easy for candidates to see which individuals and groups aided their election bids, even if the aid was indirect. According to the testimony of several former senators, this knowledge certainly influenced their actions on important policy issues. Donors who contributed large amounts to political parties and whose money aided senators' election (or reelection) bids certainly received more access to the politicians than ordinary members of the public had.

The BCRA limits expenditures as an attempt to close the soft-money loophole. It limits the amount of financial resources that can flow from parties to specific electoral contests. Parties and political action committees are therefore much less able to help particular politicians, and a donor cannot be sure his or her contributions will go to a candidate that he or she might wish to influence. However, these limits have not ended the controversy over campaign financing. The Supreme Court upheld most of BCRA in *McConnell v. Federal Election Commission (FEC)* (2003)—the case discussed in the following selections—but the dissent by Justice Antonin Scalia was unusually sharp, and the law continues to be criticized. By limiting campaign expenditures, say opponents, the Congress has violated the modern-day freedom of the press and undermined the democratic process.

Perhaps more important, wealthy donors and motivated organizations have found yet another way to get around limits on their participation in the electoral process. So-called 527 groups—named after the section of the tax code devoted to political organizations—have sprung up to advocate positions that are clearly directed for or against certain candidates, yet they remain largely unregulated. Groups such as MoveOn.org and Swift Boat Veterans for Truth have inserted themselves into elections yet remain outside of the FEC's reach. No doubt as politicians devise ever-tighter restrictions on campaign finances, more creative means of supporting candidates will be found.

> "Take away Congress' authority to regu-
> late the appearance of undue influence
> and 'the cynical assumption that large
> donors call the tune could jeopardize
> the willingness of voters to take part in
> democratic governance.'"

Majority Opinion: Limiting "Soft Money" Campaign Contributions Is Constitutional

John Paul Stevens and Sandra Day O'Connor

John Paul Stevens is the longest-serving member of the Supreme Court (as of 2009). He was appointed to the Court in 1975. The first woman appointed to the Court, Sandra Day O'Connor, served from 1981 until 2006.

This section of the majority opinion by Stevens and O'Connor focuses on the heart of the Bipartisan Campaign Reform Act (BCRA). The BCRA limited so-called soft-money contributions—money channeled through political parties rather than given directly to a candidate—to aid the campaigns of specific candidates. Candidates were aware of the sources of the soft money, and both the Democratic and Republican Parties offered "access" to candidates for sufficiently large contributions. The law's opponents claimed it violated First Amendment free-speech rights, but the Court ruled that soft money had more to do with political influence than political ideas. Congress had a legitimate

John Paul Stevens and Sandra Day O'Connor, majority opinion, *McConnell v. Federal Election Commission*, U.S. Supreme Court, December 10, 2003.

interest in restricting the amount of soft-money contributions and how they were used, the ruling held.

The core of Title I is new FECA [Federal Election Campaign Act] Section 323(a), which provides that "national committee[s] of a political party . . . may not solicit, receive, or direct to another person a contribution, donation, or transfer of funds or any other thing of value, or spend any funds, that are not subject to the limitations, prohibitions, and reporting requirements of this Act." The prohibition extends to "any officer or agent acting on behalf of such a national committee, and any entity that is directly or indirectly established, financed, or maintained, or controlled by such a national committee."

The main goal of Section 323(a) is modest. In large part, it simply effects a return to the scheme that [has been] approved . . . and that was subverted by the creation of the FEC's [Federal Election Commission's] allocation regime, which permitted the political parties to fund federal electioneering efforts with a combination of hard and soft money. Under that allocation regime, national parties were able to use vast amounts of soft money in their efforts to elect federal candidates. Consequently, as long as they directed the money to the political parties, donors could contribute large amounts of soft money for use in activities designed to influence federal elections. New Section 323(a) is designed to put a stop to that practice.

Soft-Money Ban Necessary

The Government defends Section 323(a)'s ban on national, parties' involvement with soft money as necessary to prevent the actual, and apparent corruption of federal candidates and officeholders. Our cases have made clear that the prevention of corruption or its appearance constitutes a sufficiently important interest to justify political contribution limits. We have not limited that interest to the elimination of cash-for-votes exchanges. In *Buckley*,[1] we expressly rejected the argument that antibribery laws provided a less restrictive alternative to FECA's contribution limits, noting that such laws "deal[t] with only the most blatant and specific attempts of those with money to influence government action." Thus, "[i]n speaking of 'improper influence' and 'opportunities for abuse' in addition to '*quid pro quo* [exchanging "this for that"] arrangements,' we [have] recognized a concern not confined to bribery of public officials, but extending to the broader threat from politicians too compliant with the wishes of large contributors."

Of "almost equal" importance has been the Government's interest in combating the appearance or perception of corruption engendered by large campaign contributions. Take away Congress' authority to regulate the appearance of undue influence and "the cynical assumption that large donors call the tune could jeopardize the willingness of voters to take part in democratic governance." And because the First Amendment does not require Congress to ignore the fact that "candidates, donors, and parties test the limits of the current law," these interests have been sufficient to justify not only contribution limits themselves, but laws preventing the circumvention of such limits. . . .

The question for present purposes is whether large *soft-money* contributions to national party committees have a corrupting influence or give rise to the appearance of corruption. Both common sense and the ample record in these cases confirm Congress' belief that they do. As set forth above, the FEC's allocation regime has invited widespread circumvention of FECA's limits on contributions to parties for the purpose of influencing federal elections. Under this system, corporate, union, and wealthy individual donors have been free to con-

1. *Buckley v. Valeo* (1976) upheld the campaign contribution limits of the Federal Election Campaign Act of 1971, but ruled that the campaign spending limits in the same law violated the First Amendment's guarantee of free speech.

tribute substantial sums of soft money to the national parties, which the parties can spend for the specific purpose of influencing a particular candidate's federal election. It is not only plausible, but likely, that candidates would feel grateful for such donations and that donors would seek to exploit that gratitude.

Exploiting a Loophole

The evidence in the record shows that candidates and donors alike have in fact exploited the soft-money loophole, the former to increase their prospects of election and the latter to create debt on the part of officeholders, with the national parties serving as willing intermediaries. Thus, despite FECA's hard-money Limits on direct contributions to candidates, federal officeholders have commonly asked donors to make soft-money donations to national and state committees "solely in order to assist federal campaigns," including the officeholder's own. Parties kept tallies of the amounts of soft money raised by each officeholder, and "the amount of money a Member of Congress raise[d] for the national political committees often affect[ed] the amount the committees g[a]ve to assist the Member's campaign." Donors often asked that their contributions be credited to particular candidates, and the parties obliged, irrespective of whether the funds were hard or soft. National party committees often teamed with individual candidates' campaign committees to create joint fundraising committees, which enabled the candidates to take advantage of the party's higher contribution limits while still allowing donors to give to their preferred candidate. Even when not participating directly in the fundraising, federal officeholders were well aware of the identities of the donors: National party committees would distribute lists of potential or actual donors, or donors themselves would report their generosity to officeholders.

For their part, lobbyists, CEOs [chief executive officers], and wealthy individuals alike all have candidly admitted donating substantial sums of soft money to national committees not on ideological grounds, but for the express purpose of securing influence over federal officials. For example, a former lobbyist and partner at a lobbying firm in Washington, D.C., stated in his declaration:

> You are doing a favor for somebody by making a large [soft-money] donation and they appreciate it. Ordinarily, people feel inclined to reciprocate favors. Do a bigger favor for someone—that is, write a larger check—and they feel even more compelled to reciprocate. In my experience, overt words are rarely exchanged about contributions, but people do have understandings.

Donors Pursue Influence, Not Ideology

Particularly telling is the fact that, in [the election years of] 1996 and 2000, more than half of the top 50 soft-money donors gave substantial sums to *both* major national parties, leaving room for no other conclusion but that these donors were seeking influence, or avoiding retaliation, rather than promoting any particular ideology.

The evidence from the federal officeholders' perspective is similar. For example, one former Senator described the influence purchased by nonfederal donations as follows:

> Too often, Members' first thought is not what is right or what they believe, but how it will affect fundraising. Who, after all, can seriously contend that a $100,000 donation does not alter the way one thinks about—and quite possibly votes on—an issue? ... When you don't pay the piper that finances your campaigns, you will never get any more money from that piper. Since money is the mother's milk of politics, you never want to be in that situation.

By bringing soft-money donors and federal candidates and officeholders together, "[p]arties are thus necessarily the instruments of some contributors whose object is not to support the party's message or to elect party candidates across the board, but rather to support a specific candidate for the sake of a position on one narrow issue, or even to support any candidate who will be obliged to the contributors."

Evidence of Corruption

Plaintiffs argue that without concrete evidence of an instance in which a federal officeholder has actually switched a vote (or, presumably, evidence of a specific instance where the public believes a vote was switched), Congress has not shown that there exists real or apparent corruption. But the record is to the contrary. The evidence connects soft money to manipulations of the legislative calendar, leading to Congress' failure to enact, among other things, generic drug legislation, tort reform, and tobacco legislation. To claim that such actions do not change legislative outcomes surely misunderstands the legislative process.

More importantly, plaintiffs conceive of corruption too narrowly. Our [the Supreme Court's] cases have firmly established that Congress' legitimate interest extends beyond preventing simple cash-for-votes corruption to curbing "undue influence on an officeholder's judgment, and the appearance of such influence." Many of the "deeply disturbing examples" of corruption cited by this Court in *Buckley* to justify FECA's contribution limits were not episodes of vote buying, but evidence that various corporate interests had given substantial donations to gain access to high-level government officials. Even if that access did not secure actual influence, it certainly gave the "appearance of such influence."

The record in the present case is replete with similar examples of national party committees peddling access to federal candidates and officeholders in exchange for large soft-money donations. As one former Senator put it:

Special interests who give large amounts of soft money to political parties do in fact achieve their objectives. They do get special access. Sitting Senators and House Members have limited amounts of time, but they make time available in their schedules to meet with representatives of business and unions and wealthy individuals who gave large sums to their parties. These are not idle chit-chats about the philosophy of democracy.... Senators are pressed by their benefactors to introduce legislation, to amend legislation, to block legislation, and to vote on legislation in a certain way.

So pervasive is this practice that the six national party committees actually furnish their own menus of opportunities for access to would-be soft-money donors, with increased prices reflecting an increased level of access. For example, the DCCC [Democratic Congressional Campaign Committee] offers a range of donor options, starting with the $10,000-per-year Business Forum program, and going up to the $100,000-per-year National Finance Board program. The latter entitles the donor to bimonthly conference calls with the Democratic House leadership and chair of the DCCC, complimentary invitations to all DCCC fundraising events, two private dinners with the Democratic House leadership and ranking members, and two retreats with the Democratic House leader and DCCC chair in Telluride, Colorado, and Hyannisport, Massachusetts. Similarly, "the RNC's [Republican National Committee's] donor programs offer greater access to federal office holders as the donations grow larger, with the highest level and most personal access offered to the largest soft money donors."

Corruption Not an American Value

Despite this evidence and the close ties that candidates and officeholders have with their parties, Justice [Anthony] Kennedy would limit Congress' regulatory interest *only* to the prevention of the actual or apparent *quid pro quo* corruption "inherent in" contributions made directly to, contributions made at the express behest of, and expenditures made in coordination with, a federal officeholder or candidate. Regulation of any other donation or expenditure—regardless of its size, the recipient's relationship to the candidate or officeholder, its potential impact on a candidate's election, its value to the candidate, or its unabashed and explicit intent to purchase influence—would, according to Justice Kennedy, simply be out of bounds. This crabbed view of corruption, and particularly of the appearance of corruption, ignores precedent, common sense, and the realities of political fundraising exposed by the record in this litigation.

Justice Kennedy's interpretation of the First Amendment would render Congress powerless to address more subtle but equally dispiriting forms of corruption. Just as troubling to a functioning democracy as classic *quid pro quo* corruption is the danger that officeholders will decide issues not on the merits or the desires of their constituencies, but according to the wishes of those who have made large financial contributions valued by the officeholder. Even if it occurs only occasionally, the potential for such undue influence is manifest. And unlike straight cash-for-votes transactions, such corruption is neither easily detected nor practical to criminalize. The best means of prevention is to identify and to remove the temptation. The evidence set forth above, which is but a sampling of the reams of disquieting evidence contained in the record, convincingly demonstrates that soft-money contributions to political parties carry with them just such temptation.

"In response to this assault on the free exchange of ideas . . . the Court has placed its imprimatur on these unprecedented restrictions."

Dissenting Opinion: The Court's Ruling Abandons Its Duty to Protect Political Free Speech

Clarence Thomas

Clarence Thomas was appointed to the Supreme Court by George H.W. Bush in 1991. He is the second African American to serve on the Court.

In the following excerpts from his dissent in McConnell v. Federal Election Commission, *Thomas attacks the majority's acquiescence in what he calls an "unprecedented" attack on free speech, especially on the "core" area of free speech, the exchange of political ideas. He believes Congress's "anticircumvention rationale"—the attempt to close the "soft-money" loophole in earlier campaign finance laws, will lead to continually expanding restrictions on political speech. Indeed, he sees the decision as continuing "errors" in an earlier ruling,* Buckley v. Valeo *(1976), which upheld restrictions on campaign contributions in a 1971 campaign finance law. In addition, he is skeptical of the evidence of corruption presented by the case, calling it vague and hinting that what some see as improper influence in preventing useful laws from being passed is merely sour grapes from the losing side in debates over policy.*

Clarence Thomas, dissenting opinion, *McConnell v. Federal Election Commission*, U.S. Supreme Court, December 10, 2003.

The First Amendment provides that "Congress shall make no law ... abridging the freedom of speech." Nevertheless, the Court today upholds what can only be described as the most significant abridgment of the freedoms of speech and association since the Civil War. With breathtaking scope, the Bipartisan Campaign Reform Act of 2002 (BCRA), directly targets and constricts core political speech, the "primary object of First Amendment protection." Because "the First Amendment 'has its fullest and most urgent application' to speech uttered during a campaign for political office," our duty is to approach these restrictions "with the utmost skepticism" and subject them to the "strictest scrutiny."

The Court's Hypocrisy

In response to this assault on the free exchange of ideas and with only the slightest consideration of the appropriate standard of review or of the Court's traditional role of protecting First Amendment freedoms, the Court has placed its *imprimatur* [official approval] on these unprecedented restrictions. The very "purpose of the First Amendment [is] to preserve an uninhibited marketplace of ideas in which truth will ultimately prevail." Yet today the fundamental principle that "the best test of truth is the power of the thought to get itself accepted in the competition of the market" is cast aside in the purported service of preventing "corruption," or the mere "appearance of corruption." Apparently, the marketplace of ideas is to be fully open only to defamers, nude dancers, pornographers, flag burners, and cross burners.[1]

Because I cannot agree with the treatment given by Justice [John Paul] Stevens' and Justice [Sandra Day] O'Connor's opinion (hereinafter joint opinion) to speech that is "indispensable to the effective and intelligent use of the processes of popular government to shape the destiny of modern industrial society," I respectfully dissent. . . .

1. Thomas is referring to a series of Supreme Court cases that ruled these activities to be constitutionally protected "free expression."

"[C]ampaign finance laws are subject to strict scrutiny," and thus Title I [of the BCRA] must satisfy that demanding standard even if it were (incorrectly) conceived of as nothing more than a contribution limitation. The defendants do not even attempt to defend Title I under this standard, and for good reason: The various restrictions imposed by Title I are ... narrowly tailored to target only corrupting or problematic donations. ... And, as I have previously noted, it is unclear why "[b]ribery laws [that] bar precisely the *quid pro quo* [an exchange of "this for that"] arrangements that are targeted here" and "disclosure laws" are not "less restrictive means of addressing [the Government's] interest in curtailing corruption."

Corruption Can Be Countered

The joint opinion not only continues the errors of *Buckley v. Valeo*,[2] by applying a low level of scrutiny to contribution ceilings, but also builds upon these errors by expanding the anti-circumvention rationale beyond reason.[3] Admittedly, exploitation of an anticircumvention concept has a long pedigree, going back at least to *Buckley* itself. *Buckley* upheld a $1,000 contribution ceiling as a way to combat both the "actuality and appearance of corruption." The challengers in *Buckley* contended both that bribery laws represented "a less restrictive means of dealing with 'proven and suspected *quid pro quo* arrangements,'" and that the $1,000 contribution ceiling was overbroad as "most large contributors do not seek improper influence over a candidate's position or an officeholder's action." The Court rejected the first argument on the grounds that "laws making criminal the giving and taking of bribes deal with only the most blatant and specific attempts of those

2. In *Buckley v. Valeo* (1976) the Court upheld restrictions on campaign contributions, but ruled that restrictions on campaign expenditures were an unconstitutional restriction on free speech.
3. By "anticircumvention rationale," Thomas means the government is trying to close the "soft money" loophole in the previous campaign finance law.

with money to influence governmental action," and rejected the second on the grounds that "it [is] difficult to isolate suspect contributions." But a broadly drawn bribery law would cover even subtle and general attempts to influence government officials corruptly, eliminating the Court's first concern. And, an effective bribery law would deter actual *quid pro quos* and would, in all likelihood, eliminate any appearance of corruption in the system.

Hence, at root, the *Buckley* Court was concerned that bribery laws could not be effectively enforced to prevent *quid pro quos* between donors and officeholders, and the only rational reading of *Buckley* is that it approved the $1,000 contribution ceiling on this ground. The Court then, however, having at least in part concluded that individual contribution ceilings were necessary to prevent easy evasion of bribery laws, proceeded to uphold a separate contribution limitation, using, as the only justification, the "prevent[ion] [of] evasion of the $1,000 contribution limitation." The need to prevent circumvention of a limitation that was itself an anticircumvention measure led to the upholding of another significant restriction on individuals' freedom of speech.

Anticipating Corruption

The joint opinion now repeats this process. [The] New Federal Election Campaign Act [FECA] of 1971 is intended to prevent easy circumvention of the (now) $2,000 contribution ceiling. The joint opinion even recognizes this, relying heavily on evidence that, for instance, "candidates and donors alike have in fact exploited the soft-money loophole, the former to increase their prospects of election and the latter to create debt on the part of officeholders, with the national parties serving as willing intermediaries." The joint opinion upholds Section 323(a), in part, on the grounds that it had become too easy to circumvent the $2,000 cap by using the national parties as go-betweens.

And the remaining provisions of new FECA Section 323 are upheld mostly as measures preventing circumvention of other contribution limits, including Section 323(a), which, as I have already explained, is a second-order anticircumvention measure. The joint opinion's handling of Section 323(f) is perhaps most telling, as it upholds Section 323(f) only because of "Congress' eminently reasonable *prediction* that . . . state and local candidates and officeholders will become the next conduits for the soft-money funding of sham issue advertising." That is, this Court upholds a third-order anticircumvention measure based on Congress' anticipation of circumvention of these second-order anticircumvention measures that might possibly, at some point in the future, pose some problem.

It is not difficult to see where this leads. Every law has limits, and there will always be behavior not covered by the law but at its edges; behavior easily characterized as "circumventing" the law's prohibition. Hence, speech regulation will again expand to cover new forms of "circumvention," only to spur supposed circumvention of the new regulations, and so forth. Rather than permit this never-ending and self-justifying process, I would require that the Government explain why proposed speech restrictions are needed in light of actual Government interests, and, in particular, why the bribery laws are not sufficient.

Existing Laws Are Effective

But Title I falls even on the joint opinion's terms. This Court has held that "[t]he quantum of empirical evidence needed to satisfy heightened judicial scrutiny of legislative judgments will vary up or down with the novelty and plausibility of the justification raised." And three Members of today's majority have observed that "the opportunity for corruption" presented by "[u]nregulated 'soft money' contributions" is "at best, attenuated." Such an observation is quite clearly correct. A donation to a political party is a clumsy method by which to influence a candidate, as the party is free to spend the donation however it sees fit, and could easily spend the money as to provide no help to the candidate. And, a soft-money donation to a party will be of even less benefit to a candidate, "because of legal restrictions on how the money may be spent." It follows that the defendants bear an especially heavy empirical burden in justifying Title I.

The evidence cited by the joint opinion does not meet this standard and would barely suffice for anything more than rational-basis review. The first category of the joint opinion's evidence is evidence that "federal officeholders have commonly asked donors to make soft-money donations to national and state committees solely in order to assist federal campaigns, including the officeholder's own." But to the extent that donors and federal officeholders have collaborated so that donors could give donations to a national party committee "for the purpose of influencing any election for Federal office," the alleged soft-money donation is in actuality a regular "contribution" as already defined and regulated by FECA. Neither the joint opinion nor the defendants present evidence that enforcement of pre-BCRA law has proved to be impossible, ineffective, or even particularly difficult.

The second category is evidence that "lobbyists, CEOs [chief executive officers], and wealthy individuals" have "donat[ed] substantial sums of soft money to national committees not on ideological grounds, but for the express purpose of securing influence over federal officials." Even if true (and the cited evidence consists of nothing more than vague allegations of wrongdoing), it is unclear why existing bribery laws could not address this problem. Again, neither the joint opinion nor the defendants point to evidence that the enforcement of bribery laws has been or would be ineffective. If the problem has been clear and widespread, as the joint opinion suggests, I would expect that convictions, or at least prosecutions, would be more frequent.

Evidence of Corruption Weak at Best

The third category is evidence characterized by the joint opinion as "connect[ing] soft money to manipulations of the legislative calendar, leading to Congress' failure to enact, among other things, generic drug legislation, tort reform, and tobacco legislation." But the evidence for this is no stronger than the evidence that there has been actual vote buying or vote switching for soft money. The joint opinion's citations to the record do not stand for the propositions that they claim. . . . In fact, the findings by two of the District Court's judges confirm that the evidence of any *quid pro quo* corruption is exceedingly weak, if not nonexistent. The evidence cited by the joint opinion is properly described as "at best, [the Members of Congress'] personal conjecture regarding the impact of soft money donations on the voting practices of their present and former colleagues."

The joint opinion also places a substantial amount of weight on the fact that "in 1996 and 2000, more than half of the top 50 soft-money donors gave substantial sums to *both* major national parties," and suggests that this fact "leav[es] room for no other conclusion but that these donors were seeking influence, or avoiding retaliation, rather than promoting any particular ideology." But that is not necessarily the case. The two major parties are not perfect ideological opposites, and supporters or opponents of certain policies or ideas might find substantial overlap between the two parties. If donors feel that both major parties are in general agreement over an issue of importance to them, it is unremarkable that such donors show support for both parties. This common-sense explanation surely belies the joint opinion's too-hasty conclusion drawn from a relatively innocent fact.

The Court today finds such sparse evidence sufficient.

"The first instinct of power is the retention of power, and, under a Constitution that requires periodic elections, that is best achieved by the suppression of election-time speech."

Dissenting Opinion: Limiting Campaign Expenditures Increases Incumbents' Hold on Power

Antonin Scalia

Antonin Scalia was appointed to the Supreme Court by President Ronald Reagan in 1986. He is known as a staunch conservative.

In his sharp dissent in McConnell v. Federal Election Commission, *excerpted here, Scalia makes the case that the Bipartisan Campaign Reform Act of 2002, a.k.a. the McCain-Feingold law, will protect incumbents from effective challenge. Incumbent representatives and senators have a built-in advantage in name recognition already, he argues, and limits on campaign expenditures will increase that advantage, even if limits apply to both challengers and officeholders. In debating the law, the legislators themselves emphasized that the law would help eliminate negative advertising, an effect which, Scalia says, will shield the government from criticism. In Scalia's opinion the Court acquiesced in limiting political free speech when it upheld limits on campaign contributions in the past. The Court's approval of the*

Antonin Scalia, dissenting opinion, *McConnell v. Federal Election Commission*, U.S. Supreme Court, December 10, 2003.

McCain-Feingold law's restrictions on expenditures is another giant step down the road to controlling criticism of the government, Scalia contends.

This is a sad day for the freedom of speech. Who could have imagined that the same Court which, within the past four years, has sternly disapproved of restrictions upon such inconsequential forms of expression as virtual child pornography, tobacco advertising, dissemination of illegally intercepted communications, and sexually explicit cable programming, would smile with favor upon a law that cuts to the heart of what the First Amendment is meant to protect: the right to criticize the government. For that is what the most offensive provisions of this legislation [McCain-Feingold] are all about. We are governed by Congress, and this legislation prohibits the criticism of Members of Congress by those entities most capable of giving such criticism loud voice: national political parties and corporations, both of the commercial and the not-for-profit sort. It forbids pre-election criticism of incumbents by corporations, even not-for-profit corporations, by use of their general funds; and forbids national-party use of "soft" money to fund "issue ads" that incumbents find so offensive.

A Built-in Advantage

To be sure, the legislation is evenhanded: It similarly prohibits criticism of the candidates who oppose Members of Congress in their reelection bids. But as everyone knows, this is an area in which evenhandedness is not fairness. If *all* electioneering were evenhandedly prohibited, incumbents would have an enormous advantage. Likewise, if incumbents and challengers are limited to the same quantity of electioneering, incumbents are favored. In other words, *any* restriction upon a type of campaign speech that is equally available to challengers and incumbents tends to favor incumbents.

Beyond that, however, the present legislation *targets* for prohibition certain categories of campaign speech that are particularly harmful to incumbents. Is it accidental, do you think, that incumbents raise about three times as much "hard money"[direct contributions]—the sort of funding generally *not* restricted by this legislation—as do their challengers? Or that lobbyists (who seek the favor of incumbents) give 92 percent of their money in "hard" contributions? Is it an oversight, do you suppose, that the so-called "millionaire provisions" raise the contribution limit for a candidate running against an individual who devotes to the campaign (as challengers often do) great personal wealth, but do not raise the limit for a candidate running against an individual who devotes to the campaign (as incumbents often do) a massive election "war chest"? And is it mere happenstance, do you estimate, that national-party funding, which is severely limited by the Act, is more likely to assist cash-strapped challengers than flush-with-hard-money incumbents? Was it unintended, by any chance, that incumbents are free personally to receive some soft money and even to solicit it for other organizations, while national parties are not? . . .

The Right to Hire "Gladiators"

It was said by congressional proponents of this legislation, with support from the law reviews, that since this legislation regulates nothing but the expenditure of money for speech, as opposed to speech itself, the burden it imposes is not subject to full First Amendment scrutiny; the government may regulate the raising and spending of campaign funds just as it regulates other forms of conduct, such as burning draft cards, or camping out on the National Mall. That proposition has been endorsed by one of the two authors of today's principal opinion: "The right to use one's own money to hire gladiators, [and] to fund 'speech by proxy,' . . . [are] property rights . . . not entitled to the same protection as the right to say what one pleases." Until today, however, that view has been categorically rejected by our jurisprudence. As we said in *Buckley* [*v. Valeo*] (1976), when the Court upheld restrictions on campaign contributions but not on campaign expenditures] "this Court has never suggested that the dependence of a communication on the expenditure of money operates itself to introduce a nonspeech element or to reduce the exacting scrutiny required by the First Amendment."

Our traditional view was correct, and today's cavalier attitude toward regulating the financing of speech (the "exacting scrutiny" test of *Buckley* is not uttered in any majority opinion, and is not observed in the ones from which I dissent) frustrates the fundamental purpose of the First Amendment. In any economy operated on even the most rudimentary principles of division of labor, effective public communication requires the speaker to make use of the services of others. An author may write a novel, but he will seldom publish and distribute it himself. A freelance reporter may write a story, but he will rarely edit, print, and deliver it to subscribers. To a government bent on suppressing speech, this mode of organization presents opportunities: Control any cog in the machine, and you can halt the whole apparatus. License printers, and it matters little whether authors are still free to write. Restrict the sale of books, and it matters little who prints them. Predictably, repressive regimes have exploited these principles by attacking all levels of the production and dissemination of ideas. In response to this threat, we have interpreted the First Amendment broadly.

Effective Speech Requires Money

Division of labor requires a means of mediating exchange, and in a commercial society, that means is supplied by money. The publisher pays the author for the right to sell his book; it pays its staff who print and assemble the book; it demands payments from booksellers who bring the book to market. This, too, presents opportunities for repression: Instead of regulating the various parties to the enterprise individually, the government can suppress their ability to coordinate by regulating their use of money. What good is the right to print books without a right to buy works from authors? Or the right to publish newspapers without the right to pay delivery-men? The right to speak would be largely ineffective if it did not include the right to engage in financial transactions that are the incidents of its exercise.

This is not to say that *any* regulation of money is a regulation of speech. The government may apply general commercial regulations to those who use money for speech if it applies them evenhandedly to those who use money for other purposes. But where the government singles out money used to fund speech as its legislative object, it is acting against speech as such, no less than if it had targeted the paper on which a book was printed or the trucks that deliver it to the bookstore. . . .

Protection for the Powerful

This litigation is about preventing criticism of the government. I cannot say for certain that many, or some, or even any, of the Members of Congress who voted for this legislation did so not to produce "fairer" campaigns, but to mute criticism of their records and facilitate reelection. Indeed, I will stipulate that all those who voted for the Act believed they were acting for the good of the country. There remains the problem of the Charlie Wilson Phenomenon, named after Charles Wilson, former president of General Motors, who is supposed to have said during the Senate hearing on his nomination as Secretary of Defense that "what's good for General Motors is good for the country." Those in power, even giving them the benefit of the greatest good will, are inclined to believe that what is good for them is good for the country. Whether in prescient recognition of the Charlie Wilson Phenomenon, or out of fear of good old-fashioned, malicious, self-interested manipulation, "[t]he fundamental approach of the First Amendment . . . was to assume the worst, and to rule the regulation of political speech 'for fairness' sake' simply out of bounds." Having abandoned that approach to a limited extent in *Buckley*, we abandon it much further today.

We will unquestionably be called upon to abandon it further still in the future. The most frightening passage in the lengthy floor debates on this legislation is the following assurance given by one of the cosponsoring Senators to his colleagues:

> This is a modest step, it is a first step, it is an essential step, but it does not even begin to address, in some ways, the fundamental problems that exist with the hard money aspect of the system.

A Grim Outlook for Free Speech

The system indeed. The first instinct of power is the retention of power, and, under a Constitution that requires periodic elections, that is best achieved by the suppression of election-time speech. We have witnessed merely the second scene of Act I of what promises to be a lengthy tragedy. In scene 3 the Court, having abandoned most of the First Amendment weaponry that *Buckley* left intact, will be even less equipped to resist the incumbents' writing of the rules of political debate. The federal election campaign laws, which are already (as today's opinions show) so voluminous, so detailed, so complex, that no ordinary citizen dare run for office, or even contribute a significant sum, without hiring an expert advisor in the field, can be expected to grow more voluminous, more detailed, and more complex in the years to come—and always, always, with the objective of reducing the excessive amount of speech.

> "It is difficult to represent the little fellow when the big fellow pays the tab."

Large Campaign Contributors Buy Access to Politicians

Mark Green

Mark Green, a public interest lawyer, is president of the liberal talk-radio network Air America.

In this piece, written before the passage of the Bipartisan Campaign Reform Act (also known as McCain-Feingold), Green presents the startling reality of political money and its influence on the democratic process. According to the testimony of senators and representatives, there is no way of getting around their feeling beholden to large contributors. Outright bribery is rare, but politicians are perfectly aware when they vote that they may be helping or hurting a major benefactor. According to Green, this is the reason so many policies supported by the American people fail to pass Congress. He is hopeful, however, that the McCain-Feingold legislation will be effective in the fight against the influence of money on politics.

Among the least-discussed numbers from [election day] November 5 [2002] is $184 million—the amount by which Republican national committees out-spent their Democratic equivalents. And with President [George W.] Bush loudly beating his war drums [to invade Iraq], who heard any discussion about the escalating cost of campaigns? Spending in the New York and Pennsylvania gubernatorial elections, for example, *tripled* within one election cycle.

Mark Green, "The Evil of Access," *The Nation*, December 30, 2002. Copyright © 2002 by The Nation Magazine/The Nation Company, Inc. Reproduced by permission.

The evidence that money shouts is mountainous: Ninety-four percent of the time, the bigger-spending Congressional candidate wins—and 98 percent of House incumbents win. The average price of a House seat rose from $87,000 in 1976 to $840,000 in 2000. It cost Ken Livingstone 80 cents a vote to win the London mayoralty [in 2001], compared with Michael Bloomberg's $100 a vote in New York City.

Special Interests Get Special Access

As money metastasizes throughout our political process, the erosion of our democracy should be evident to left and right alike.

While members publicly and indignantly deny that big contributions often come with strings attached, all privately concede the obvious mutual shakedown—or as one Western senator told me, "Senators are human calculators who can weigh how much money every vote will cost them." Two who violated the usual senatorial *omertá* [the vow of "silence or death" taken by mafia members] gave dispositions in the federal district court arguments on the McCain-Feingold law. "Who, after all, can seriously contend," said former Senator Alan Simpson, "that a $100,000 donation does not alter the way one thinks about—and quite possibly votes on—an issue?" Senator Zell Miller bluntly described the daily conversations from fundraising cubicles: "I'd remind the agribusinessman I was on the Agriculture Committee; I'd remind the banker I was on the Banking Committee. . . . Most large contributors understand only two things: what you can do for them and what you can do to them. I always left that room feeling like a cheap prostitute who'd had a busy day." The access that money buys, of course, doesn't guarantee legislative success, but the lack of it probably guarantees failure.

After [the] 9/11 [2001, terrorist attacks], for example, many legislators thought the argument for energy conservation and reduced dependence on Middle Eastern oil was obvious. So Senators John Kerry and John McCain were stunned when their effort to increase fuel-efficiency standards failed 62 to 38—with the average no vote getting $18,000 in donations from auto companies and the average yes vote only $6,000. One senator insisting on anonymity said: "That vote was one of the most politically cowardly things I ever saw in the Senate. We know how to be energy-efficient, and it starts with cars."

Fundraising Is a Time Thief

Imagine if someone kidnapped all candidates for state and federal office for half of each day. The story would be bigger than Gary Condit,[1] and would surely lead to calls for tougher penalties against political kidnapping.

Well, there is such a culprit. It's the current system of financing political campaigns, which pits each candidate in a spiraling "arms race," not merely to raise enough money but to raise far more than any rival. One Midwestern senator complained, "Senators used to be here Monday through Friday; now we're lucky to be in mid-Tuesday to Thursday, because Mondays and Fridays are for fundraisers. Also, members loathe voting on controversial issues, because it'll be used against you when you're raising money."

Candidates start to feel like Bill Murray in [the film] *Groundhog Day*, trapped in a daily, stultifying repetition they can't escape. As a [New York City] mayoral candidate I made 30,000 phone calls (that is not a misprint) over two years to lists of potential donors and spoke at 205 of my own fundraising events. It's hard to overstate the physical and psychological stamina required in such an effort, and how little time and energy it leaves for all else.

Potential candidates know they have to succeed in not one but two elections: The first, in which contributors "vote" with

1. Gary Condit was a representative who became news in 2001 when a young female intern from his office went missing. Her body was eventually found; nothing ever connected Condit to the disappearance or murder.

their dollars, comes long before constituents have their say. And if you don't win round one financially, you might as well not bother with round two; after all, because incumbency attracts money and money entrenches incumbency, no challenger spending under $850,000 won a House seat in 2000. With odds like those, many talented women and men flinch.

Pay to Play

Most Republicans oppose new regulations and taxes out of authentic belief. So they regard the special-interest funding of public elections as a brilliant system: For them, principles and payments go hand in hand. Robert Reich, a former Labor Secretary and recent Massachusetts gubernatorial candidate, believes his party is losing its identity as the champion of the average family "because Democrats became dependent on the rich to finance their campaigns. It is difficult to represent the little fellow when the big fellow pays the tab."

Ever wonder why polls show that so many Americans strongly favor higher minimum wages, prescription drug benefits for Medicare, quality daycare, publicly financed Congressional campaigns and stronger environmental protection, even at the cost of higher taxes—yet the political system can't produce any of these? The pay-to-play system is a circuit breaker between popular will and public policy.

So although issues like terrorism, healthcare and pollution absorb far more public attention and concern, the scandal of strings-attached money corrupting politics and government is the most urgent domestic problem in America today—because it makes it harder to solve nearly all our other problems. How can we produce smart defense, environmental and health policies if arms contractors, oil firms and HMOs [health maintenance organizations] have such a hammerlock on the committees charged with considering reforms? The culprit is not corrupt candidates but a corrupt system that coerces good people to take tainted money.

The old and much-discussed saga of political money may reach a climax between now [2002] and 2004 as a result of three epic developments:

First, the corporate scandals of 2001–2 started with questions about corrupt financing practices and then moved to questions about corrupt political practices. Joan Claybrook, head of Public Citizen and a veteran of the campaign finance wars, says, "Political money from the Enrons [an energy company that went bankrupt in 2001] and others bought loopholes, exemptions, lax law enforcement, underfunded regulatory agencies and the presumption that corporate officials could buy anything they wanted with the shareholders' money." Once the current war fever abates electorally, will the Enron/Adelphia/Global Crossing/Tyco/WorldCom scandals lead to a shift in our political zeitgeist, as corruption a century ago led to the Progressive Era?

Removing Congess's "For Sale" Sign

Second, the McCain-Feingold fight re-educated the public about money in politics. Given all the problems of our current system, the McCain-Feingold law is like throwing a ten-foot rope to a drowning swimmer forty feet offshore. But it's necessary to stop huge soft-money federal gifts that enable big interests to make an end run around federal bans on corporate and labor donations.

Third, the Supreme Court will likely rule next spring [2003] on the constitutionality of McCain-Feingold's two major provisions: banning soft-money fundraising by the national parties and restricting soft money for sham "issue" ads. This will be the Court's first major consideration of campaign finance since 1976's disastrous *Buckley v. Valeo* ruling, which held that legislatively enacted "expenditure limits" were an unconstitutional infringement on speech. If the Court had reached a different conclusion then, there would be no $2 million House candidates today, no $15 million Senate candidates, no $74 million mayoral candidates. [Editor's note: The Court did rule in favor of the bill's constitutionality.]

Moreover, the State of Vermont [in 2000] enacted a spending ceiling. The Court of Appeals for the Second Circuit initially upheld the law, arguing that evidence of legislators routinely selling access showed the law was a constitutionally permissible way of stopping such corruption. If this case goes to the Supreme Court with McCain-Feingold—and swing Justices Sandra Day O'Connor and Anthony Kennedy agree with the Second Circuit majority—we'll be close to taking the for-sale sign off our democracy.

Meanwhile, can the political process significantly reform not just the soft-money but also the hard-money system?

Most senators and representatives I interviewed thought Congress had exhausted itself in the McCain-Feingold fight and that this Republican Congress had no interest in going further. However, Fred Wertheimer of the campaign-reform group Democracy 21, citing the revolution of rising expectations, believes that "winning McCain-Feingold will open the door to another round," if not in this Republican Congress then in a future one.

"Congress and the country are on the brink of deciding between unlimited contributions in politics or unlimited regulation of politics."

Campaign Finance Law Should Not Target Advocacy Groups

Jonathan Rauch

Jonathan Rauch is a columnist for the National Journal *and a contributing editor for* The Atlantic.

In the following viewpoint, Rauch argues that political donations are making their way toward new types of groups in the wake of the McCain-Feingold restrictions on "soft money"— political campaign contributions given indirectly to a candidate or incumbent through his or her party organizations. Private political organizations called 527 groups, after the section of the tax code under which they are incorporated, sometimes focus on issues that can be damaging to specific political candidates, Rauch contends. For example, during the 2004 presidential campaign the Swift Boat Veterans for Truth questioned Democratic candidate John Kerry's military record. Rauch, writing in 2005, points to the danger that, in an attempt to plug loopholes in the campaign finance regulations, Congress will begin with the 527s and regulate more and more groups involved in political advocacy.

Jonathan Rauch, "Social Studies: Here's a New Campaign Finance Reform Plan: Just Stop," *National Journal*, May 7, 2005. Copyright © 2005 National Journal. Reproduced by permission.

M ost Americans outside Washington, lucky souls, have no idea what a "527" group is. The country paid no attention [in May 2005] when the Senate Rules Committee voted out a bill that would subject 527 groups to some of the same soft-money restrictions that apply to party committees. The change was portrayed by many of its advocates as little more than a technical adjustment to the existing campaign finance rules: "statutory coordination," as one expert said in Senate testimony. Asleep yet?

Wake up. This is no mere tweak. The 527 question brings campaign finance law face to face with a choice it hoped never to have to make. Congress and the country are on the brink of deciding between unlimited contributions in politics or unlimited regulation of politics.

The McCain-Feingold campaign finance reform law (officially, the Bipartisan Campaign Reform Act) was signed into law in March 2002. The Supreme Court upheld and unleashed it in December 2003. Only one election cycle has passed since then. Yet Congress is already working on new restrictions. This might reflect, as proponents of the new restrictions argue, that conditions change rapidly in the political world. Or it might suggest, as opponents retort, that the law itself is radically unstable. Unfortunately, both sides are right.

A New Type of Political Group

A 527 group is a private, tax-exempt political organization set up under Section 527 of the U.S. tax code. Such groups have been around for years but never took center stage until 2004, when they became major players. That's because McCain-Feingold shut the door on unlimited contributions (so-called "soft money") to political parties, so that many of the big-dollar donations began flowing to 527 groups instead. Some of the groups were established by partisan operatives and acted as virtual proxies for the parties (mainly the Democrats). Others—notably Swift Boat Veterans for Truth, which attacked

[2004 Democratic presidential candidate] Sen. John Kerry's Vietnam War record—made lots of people hopping mad.

According to the Campaign Finance Institute, contributions to 527 groups more than doubled between 2002 and 2004, to $405 million. Most of the money came from individuals, often in eye-popping sums; 70 percent of the total came from just 52 people who gave between $1 million and $24 million. Democratic zillionaires Peter B. Lewis and George Soros gave $16 million and $12 million respectively. This was big money if the phrase means anything at all.

Fred Wertheimer, the president of Democracy 21 (an advocacy group that says it works "to eliminate the undue influence of big money in American politics"), argues that 2004 was just the beginning. In 2006, he says, 527 groups will begin pouring money into contested House and Senate races. "Given the opportunity, this will grow and grow in future elections, and it will create enormous inequities." He is probably right. Absent further change, 527 groups will become the outlet of choice for unlimited political contributions.

On the other hand, banning soft-money donations to 527 groups would confirm the campaign finance law's transformation into an engine of unlimited political regulation. Imagine a runaway lawnmower munching every flower bed and hillock in sight, and you have an idea of what the law is at risk of becoming.

Spending money to buy ads or turn out voters is a form of political expression. At least until recently, standard legal doctrine held that such political expression could be restricted only to prevent "corruption or the appearance of corruption," as the Supreme Court ruled in 1976. But what is corruption? It's easy to see why giving $1 million directly to a politician or party might smell of bribery or extortion, but McCain-Feingold put a stop to that. Harder to see is why giving $1 million to an independent group, such as the Sierra Club or the National Rifle Association, would corrupt anybody. After all, private groups are in no position to offer legislative favors or snake down constituents.

Influence *Is* Corruption

Ordinarily, one might suppose it to be a good thing when rich people finance political mobilization and discussion. Where, exactly, is the harm in George Soros's giving $12 million to an independent political outfit that seeks to defeat President [George W.] Bush? In a recent fact sheet, Democracy 21 and the Campaign Legal Center reply this way:

> Large donations to 527 groups spending money to influence federal elections can buy influence with federal candidates, even if the 527 groups are operating independently. Since such 527 groups are spending money to elect federal candidates, and since the source and amounts of these unlimited contributions are readily available to the candidates, the contributions can buy influence with the federal candidates benefiting from the expenditures by the 527 groups.

In other words, the problem is not corruption, at least not as traditionally understood; the problem is influence. In yet other words, influence *is* corruption. And in yet other words, because politics is all about influence, *politics* is corruption—at least until all contributions to political causes are so small that politicians won't feel particularly grateful to anybody.

It is true that some of the biggest 527 groups in 2004 were partisan spin-offs; that was a predictable consequence of placing new limits on parties. But most 527 groups are genuinely independent. The Sierra Club's 527 group, for example, raised and spent $6.2 million on voter-education and get-out-the-vote efforts in 2004. If contributions were limited, "our guess is our program would probably be reduced by 90 percent," says Aimee Tavares, the Sierra Club's political operations director.

New Targets for Restrictions

The Sierra Club is one of many nonprofit advocacy groups opposing new limits on 527 groups. Some, like the Sierra Club, operate their own 527s; many do not understand how restricting political speech and voter mobilization helps democracy or cleanses politics; and many fear that once 527 groups are regulated, nonpartisan advocacy groups—the so-called 501(c)(4) groups that form the backbone of citizen advocacy—will be the next to face new restrictions.

Public Citizen has already called for a crackdown on 501 groups, saying in a press release [in] September [2004], "These new stealth PACs [political action committees] should not be allowed to operate with such impunity." Other campaign finance reformers disagree—for now. "You simply will not see the same kinds of things happen" with 501 groups as with 527 groups, Wertheimer says. But when asked whether he would rule out action against 501(c)(4) groups, Wertheimer said, "I would, based on now. If, down the road, people concluded there were massive abuses going on, I assume it would be looked at."

Many reformers say they are merely trying to prevent circumvention of the existing campaign finance law, but that is not really reassuring. "The problem," says Robert F. Bauer, a Democratic campaign finance lawyer with the firm of Perkins Coie, "is that once you have become obsessed with so-called circumvention, with the purity of the reform effort and anything that appears to threaten it, inevitably you have an endless law enforcement patrol that fans out over the countryside looking for fugitives from justice."

If soft money is blocked from 527 groups, much of it may flow to 501 groups. Once 501s' funding is restricted, then individuals' political activities may be regulated. (If George Soros buys too much influence by giving $12 million to a political organization, why let him spend the money himself?) Then the media. (Broadcasts and editorials surely influence elections.) Untethered to any reasonably circumscribed definition of corruption, the law is not just on a slippery slope; the law *is* a slippery slope.

Just Stop the Slippage

Here is another plan: Stop. Just stop.

Stop and live with McCain-Feingold for a little while. In law, stability is an important value in and of itself. Stop and ponder true campaign finance reform, which one more layer of legalistic regulation decidedly is not. Interesting proposals include partial or total deregulation; public financing of campaigns through government subsidies or personal vouchers; creating a system for anonymous donations; and hybrids of the above.

Above all, stop and insist that those who want tighter restrictions on 527s tell us: Where do *they* propose to stop? "I think we have a right to know at what point people can participate in politics without the FEC [Federal Election Commission] coming after them," says Bradley A. Smith, a member of the Federal Election Commission. Can advocates of new restrictions name even one kind of person, organization, or political activity that they believe should be unconditionally off-limits to campaign finance regulators? If they are not required to answer that question now, chances are they never will be.

CHAPTER 4

Expanding the Federal Government's Right to Prosecute Local Corruption

Case Overview

Sabri v. United States (2004)

In 2001 Minneapolis real estate developer Basim Omar Sabri was seeking permits to build a hotel and shopping center in the Eighth Ward of the city. He sought the assistance of city councilman Brian Herron in gaining approval of the project—offering the official a bribe as an inducement. In addition, Sabri paid Herron to threaten current owners of property on the proposed building site with seizure of their land by the city if they did not sell. Finally Sabri offered Herron a kickback of 10 percent for help in obtaining redevelopment grants worth around eight hundred thousand dollars. As Herron was a commissioner on the Minneapolis Community Development Agency, he was in a good position to obtain these grants.

Typically this sort of corruption would be prosecuted by local or state officials. However, in the *Sabri* case the federal prosecutor stepped in, charging Sabri under a federal anticorruption measure. The law, 18 U.S. Code Section 666(a)(2), makes it a federal crime to offer a bribe of more than five thousand dollars to any official of any city, county, state, or tribal government that receives more than ten thousand dollars' worth of federal funds yearly. In practice this means that the law applies to the overwhelming majority of local officials throughout the country.

Sabri was convicted. He appealed the conviction arguing against the federal anticorruption law on two fronts. First, he contended that the text of Section 666(a)(2) required a direct link between the corruption and the federal funds received by the local government. As the development project and funds sought were strictly local matters, said Sabri, the federal anticorruption statute did not apply. His second angle was that if the law did apply to all activities of a local government, not just the federally funded ones, the measure itself was unconstitutional. In making a federal case out of local corruption, Congress had exceeded the bounds of its authority by violating a basic principle of federalism—that local and state governments had the right to act in certain spheres without federal interference.

Sabri won at the first stage of the appeal, with the Minnesota district court agreeing that Congress had overstepped its authority. He lost at the circuit court of appeals level, however. The government prevailed by arguing that Congress's power under the spending clause of the Constitution, combined with the "necessary and proper" clause, gave Congress the right both to grant money to local governments and broad power to oversee the use of federal dollars.

The Supreme Court agreed to hear the case in order to resolve splits in opinion among lower courts, some of which had ruled Section 666(a)(2) was unconstitutional. Writing for a unanimous Court, Justice David Souter held that Congress had a right to safeguard its expenditures on local governments. Since money is fungible—that is, it can be easily transferred from one use to another—corruption in one area of a local government would, in effect, take money from those areas that the federal government was subsidizing. Moreover, the presence of corrupt officials made it likely that the government in question was poorly run, thus limiting the effectiveness of federal funds. Congress, ruled the Court, has the right to safeguard against this eventuality.

While the decision was greeted with approval by anti-corruption campaigners, those who believed in strong state and local governments saw the ruling as dangerous. These skeptics claim that making virtually all governments—state, county, and city—possible subjects of federal investigation for strictly local cases amounts to a vast expansion of federal powers.

> *"Section 666(a)(2) [of the federal anti-corruption law] upsets the delicate balance between federal and state authority that animates our Constitution."*

The Circuit Court's Dissenting Opinion: Federal Government Prosecution of Local Corruption Is Improper

Kermit Bye

Kermit Bye was nominated to the Eighth Circuit Court of Appeals by President Bill Clinton in 1999.

McCulloch v. Maryland *(1819) established Congress's power to make legislation* necessary *to pursue the national interest. However, such legislation must also be* proper *in the sense of not usurping functions that rightfully belong to state or local governments under America's system of federalism, argues Bye in the following dissenting opinion in the appeals court decision in* United States v. Sabri *(2003). Bye makes the case that the federal anticorruption statute, U.S. Constitution Section 666(a)(2), is an* improper *extension of Congress's power. In practice the law makes a federal case of bribery or attempted bribery of any local or state official. Bye believes that local law enforcement is properly left to local authorities, a practice rooted in the Constitution and reinforced by recent Supreme Court decisions. The case went on to the Supreme Court, which upheld the circuit's ruling.*

Kermit Bye, dissenting opinion, *United States v. Sabri*, Eighth Circuit Court of Appeals, April 7, 2003.

No one doubts the constitutional authority of Congress to enact criminal laws punishing behavior affecting tangible federal interests. However, when Congress seeks to punish conduct with no connection to federal interests, conduct traditionally punished only by state and local governments exercising their general police powers, Congress exceeds its constitutional authority. The statute we review today, 18 U.S.C. Section 666(a)(2), punishes a broad swath of conduct bearing little relationship to any federal interest. It establishes federal criminal liability for those who bribe state and local government officials, provided only that the government receives $10,000 per year in federal program benefits. A briber need not handle, manage, administer or supervise the receipt or disbursement of federal funds, and the purpose of the bribe need not relate to federal program benefits. It is therefore logically and legally untenable to assert a federal interest in punishing these bribers.

The Court's Decision Is Improper

In my view, the majority's decision to uphold Section 666(a)(2) despite this infirmity swims against the tide of governing law. A wave of recent Supreme Court decisions emphasizes Congress' limited ability to federalize criminal conduct, and to interfere in matters traditionally left to state governance. These decisions guide my review of Section 666(a)(2) and require my respectful dissent. . . .

The majority apparently casts aside its earlier qualm that Section 666(a)(2) requires no connection between the bribe and federal benefits. The majority instead perceives a bare, "rational relationship" between punishing bribers and maintaining the integrity of federal programs, and on that basis declares the Necessary and Proper Clause a proper font of congressional authority. This may be correct, but it answers only half the question we must decide.

In my view, the principal defect in the majority opinion is its inattention to the conjunctive "and" that separates the words "necessary and proper." The majority advances several arguments suggesting Section 666(a)(2) is "necessary," in the sense envisioned in *M'Culloch v. Maryland* (1819) [which ruled that a state cannot tax or interfere with a federal bank operating within that state]. But the majority fails to ask—let alone resolve—whether the statute is also "proper." This is not merely a semantic dispute, for in *Printz* [*v. United States* (1997), which limits federal power over state and local police officers] and *Alden* [*v. Maine* (1999), which limits congressional authority by protecting states' sovereign immunity in their respective courts] the Supreme Court advanced an interpretation of "proper" that calls into question the constitutionality of federal statutes that trespass upon the domain of state and local legislative power. Section 666(a)(2) is one such statute.

M'Culloch holds that Congress enjoys broad powers to select the means of enacting its objectives. Thus, in determining whether a law is "necessary," courts must review Congress' law-making efforts with considerable deference. The majority describes this deference in terms of rationality: courts may not demand of Congress anything more than a rational relationship between its chosen means and ends. This reading of *M'Culloch* is, of course, received wisdom. Applying *M'Culloch* in this fashion, the majority makes a fairly convincing argument that the "fit" between Section 666(a)(2) and Congress' underlying objective to preserve the integrity of federal programs is rational. However, because there is a rational relationship between Congress' aim and the law it enacted, under *M'Culloch*, the law is "necessary." But *M'Culloch* says very little, if anything, about what makes a law "proper." That specific question largely evaded the Court's attention until *Printz* and *Alden*. . . .

Distinction Between *Necessary* and *Proper*

Printz rejected the argument that Congress could commandeer state officials to implement certain federal mandates by using its Necessary and Proper Clause power to effectuate its Commerce Clause authority. Relying solely on its understanding of what constitutes a "proper" law, the Court held [that] the Necessary and Proper Clause forbids Congress from enacting legislation that intrudes on state sovereignty.

> When a "La[w] . . . for carrying into Execution" the Commerce Clause violates the principle of state sovereignty reflected in [the Constitution,] it is not a "La[w] . . . *proper* for carrying into Execution the Commerce Clause," and is thus, in the words of The Federalist, "merely [an] ac[t] of usurpation" which "deserve[s] to be treated as such."

Like *Printz*, *Alden* recognized [that] the word "proper" restricts the scope of legislative power. *Alden* continued the Court's analysis of "proper" laws by rejecting the argument that the Necessary and Proper Clause conferred authority on Congress to subject unconsenting states to suit in state court "as a means of achieving objectives otherwise within the scope of the enumerated powers."

The Court's analysis in *Printz* and *Alden* rested entirely upon the propriety of a statute, not whether that statute was necessary. A law is "proper," the Court maintained, if it respects both the Constitution's limits on federal power and its grants of power to the states and the people. These cases teach us that a law is "proper" for the enforcement of an enumerated power only if it hews to constitutional principles of limited federal government and state sovereignty. Federal laws that usurp the traditional domain of state authority are therefore not "proper."

Respecting States' Powers

I believe Section 666(a)(2) lies outside the guideposts erected in *Printz* and *Alden* for assessing a "proper" law. The statute intrudes upon state and local concerns by federalizing anticorruption law, which is traditionally the domain of state and local legislation. Section 666(a)(2) thereby offends the Constitution's basic limitations on federal power. The only possible relationship between Section 666(a)(2) and federal interests is the sum of $10,000 in federal benefits received each year by state or local governments. There is scarcely any limit to this relationship, however. Even under a narrow view of "federal benefits," it is beyond dispute that every state—and nearly every county, tribe and city—receives that sum in yearly federal benefits. Moreover, the statute requires no connection between those federal benefits and the bribe. The lack of any connection makes all too real the risk that federal anticorruption efforts will swamp state and local efforts to combat bribery. . . .

I recognize, of course, Section 666(a)(2) does not preempt state or local power to punish corruption. Even though Section 666(a)(2) lacks preemptive effect, the sheer size and funding of the federal government's criminal justice machinery suggests the possibility of state and local anticorruption efforts dwindling. It blinks at reality to believe Section 666(a)(2) does no more than provide an additional weapon in the anticorruption arsenal. By inserting itself into a domain traditionally reserved for state and local prosecutions, the federal government treats state governments, for example, not with the respect and dignity due them as "residuary sovereigns and joint participants in the Nation's governance," but as untrustworthy organs incapable of policing their own. The development and enforcement of sound ethical standards, and of political accountability to citizens for failing to do so, lies at the very heart of sovereignty.

Section 666(a)(2) upsets the delicate balance between federal and state authority that animates our Constitution. "Congress has no more power to punish theft from the beneficiaries of its largesse than it has to punish theft from anyone else. . . . The Constitution does not contemplate that federal regulatory power should tag along after federal money like a hungry dog."

> *"The question is whether 18 U.S.C. Section 666(a)(2), proscribing bribery of state, local, and tribal officials of entities that receive at least $10,000 in federal funds, is a valid exercise of congressional authority under Article I of the Constitution. We hold that it is."*

Majority Opinion: The Federal Government May Safeguard Its Expenditures by Prosecuting Corrupt Local Officials

David Souter

David Souter was nominated for the Supreme Court by President George H.W. Bush in 1990 after serving only a few months as an appeals judge, earning him the nickname "the stealth justice" from the media. He served on the Court until 2009.

Writing for a unanimous court, Souter upholds a section of federal law—18 U.S. Constitution Section 666(a)(2)—that permits the federal government to prosecute bribery of local officials if they hold office for a municipality, county, state, or tribal authority that receives federal moneys of more than ten thousand dollars. Souter argues that Congress's constitutional power to spend money for the common good, and its power to see that such expenditures are carried out effectively, allows it to pass laws that serve to safeguard federal money. These include laws

David Souter, majority opinion, *Sabri v. United States*, U.S. Supreme Court, May 17, 2004.

that help root out corrupt local officials, even if their corrupt activities do not directly involve federal dollars.

The question is whether 18 U.S.C. Section 666(a)(2), proscribing bribery of state, local, and tribal officials of entities that receive at least $10,000 in federal funds, is a valid exercise of congressional authority under Article I of the Constitution. We hold that it is.

The Facts of the Case

Petitioner Basim Omar Sabri is a real estate developer who proposed to build a hotel and retail structure in the city of Minneapolis. Sabri lacked confidence, however, in his ability to adapt to the lawful administration of licensing and zoning laws, and offered three separate bribes to a city councilman, Brian Herron, according to the grand jury indictment that gave rise to this case. At the time the bribes were allegedly offered (between July 2, 2001, and July 17, 2001), Herron served as a member of the Board of Commissioners of the Minneapolis Community Development Agency (MCDA), a public body created by the city council to fund housing and economic development within the city.

Count 1 of the indictment charged Sabri with offering a $5,000 kickback for obtaining various regulatory approvals, and according to Count 2, Sabri offered Herron a $10,000 bribe to set up and attend a meeting with owners of land near the site Sabri had in mind, at which Herron would threaten to use the city's eminent domain authority to seize their property if they were troublesome to Sabri. Count 3 alleged that Sabri offered Herron a commission of 10% on some $800,000 in community economic development grants that Sabri sought from the city, the MCDA, and other sources.

The charges were brought under 18 U.S.C. Section 666(a)(2), which imposes federal criminal penalties on anyone who corruptly gives, offers, or agrees to give anything of value to any person, with intent to influence or reward an agent of an organization or of a State, local or Indian tribal government, or any agency thereof, in connection with any business, transaction, or series of transactions of such organization, government, or agency involving anything of value of $5,000 or more.

For criminal liability to lie, the statute requires that

the organization, government, or agency receiv[e], in any one year period, benefits in excess of $10,000 under a Federal program involving a grant, contract, subsidy, loan, guarantee, insurance, or other form of Federal assistance.

In 2001, the City Council of Minneapolis administered about $29 million in federal funds paid to the city, and in the same period, the MCDA received some $23 million of federal money. . . .

Laws to Protect Federal Expenditures

Sabri raises what he calls a facial challenge to Section 666(a)(2): the law can never be applied constitutionally because it fails to require proof of any connection between a bribe or kickback and some federal money. It is fatal, as he sees it, that the statute does not make the link an element of the crime, to be charged in the indictment and demonstrated beyond a reasonable doubt. Thus, Sabri claims his attack meets the demanding standard set out in *United States v. Salerno* [which gives federal authority to detain arrestees prior to trial only if clear and convincing evidence proves them to be dangerous] (1987), since he says no prosecution can satisfy the Constitution under this statute, owing to its failure to require proof that its particular application falls within Congress's jurisdiction to legislate. . . .

Congress has authority under the Spending Clause [of the Constitution] to appropriate federal monies to promote the general welfare, and it has corresponding authority under the Necessary and Proper Clause to see to it that taxpayer dollars appropriated under that power are in fact spent for the general welfare, and not frittered away in graft or on projects undermined when funds are siphoned off or corrupt public officers are derelict about demanding value for dollars. Congress does not have to sit by and accept the risk of operations thwarted by local and state improbity. Section 666(a)(2) addresses the problem at the sources of bribes, by rational means, to safeguard the integrity of the state, local, and tribal recipients of federal dollars.

It is true, just as Sabri says, that not every bribe or kickback offered or paid to agents of governments covered by Section 666(b) will be traceably skimmed from specific federal payments, or show up in the guise of a *quid pro quo* [exchange of "this for that"] for some dereliction in spending a federal grant. But this possibility portends no enforcement beyond the scope of federal interest, for the reason that corruption does not have to be that limited to affect the federal interest. Money is fungible, bribed officials are untrustworthy stewards of federal funds, and corrupt contractors do not deliver dollar-for-dollar value. Liquidity is not a financial term for nothing; money can be drained off here because a federal grant is pouring in there. And officials are not any the less threatening to the objects behind federal spending just because they may accept general retainers. It is certainly enough that the statutes condition the offense on a threshold amount of federal dollars defining the federal interest, such as that provided here, and on a bribe that goes well beyond liquor and cigars. . . .

Other Precedents Do Not Apply

Petitioner presses two more particular arguments against the constitutionality of Section 666(a)(2), neither of which helps him. First, he says that Section 666 is all of a piece with the legislation that a majority of this Court held to exceed Congress's authority under the Commerce Clause in *United States v. Lopez* (1995), and *United States v. Morrison* (2000). But these precedents do not control here. In *Lopez* and *Morrison*, the Court struck down federal statutes regulating gun possession near schools and gender-motivated violence, respectively, because it found the effects of those activities on interstate commerce insufficiently robust. The Court emphasized the noneconomic nature of the regulated conduct, commenting on the law at issue in *Lopez*, for example, "that by its terms [it] has nothing to do with 'commerce' or any sort of economic enterprise, however broadly one might define those terms." The Court rejected the Government's contentions that the gun law was valid Commerce Clause legislation because guns near schools ultimately bore on social prosperity and productivity, reasoning that on that logic, Commerce Clause authority would effectively know no limit. In order to uphold the legislation, the Court concluded, it would be necessary "to pile inference upon inference in a manner that would bid fair to convert congressional authority under the Commerce Clause to a general police power of the sort retained by the States."

A Watchful Federal Eye

No piling is needed here to show that Congress was within its prerogative to protect spending objects from the menace of local administrators on the take. The power to keep a watchful eye on expenditures and on the reliability of those who use public money is bound up with congressional authority to spend in the first place, and Sabri would be hard pressed to claim, in the words of the *Lopez* Court, that Section 666(a)(2) "has nothing to do with" the congressional spending power.

Sabri next argues that Section 666(a)(2) amounts to an unduly coercive, and impermissibly sweeping, condition on the grant of federal funds. . . . This is not so. Section 666(a)(2) is authority to bring federal power to bear directly on individuals who convert public spending into unearned private gain, not a means for bringing federal economic might to bear on a State's own choices of public policy.

> "I find questionable the scope the Court gives to the Necessary and Proper Clause as applied to Congress' authority to spend."

Concurring Opinion: The *Sabri* Decision Represents an Unwarranted Expansion of the "Necessary and Proper" Clause

Clarence Thomas

Clarence Thomas was nominated to the Supreme Court by George H.W. Bush in 1991. He is considered a conservative.

In his concurring opinion, excerpted here, Thomas ultimately agrees with the majority's decision in the Sabri v. United States *case; however, he disagrees with how it arrived at the decision, through what he sees as an expansion of the meaning of the "necessary and proper" clause of the Constitution in Justice David Souter's opinion. Souter holds that the important case* McCulloch v. Maryland *(1819) established that Congress has the right to make laws that are "rational means" to carry out its powers as enumerated in the Constitution. Justice Thomas disagrees, saying that John Marshall, who wrote the* McCulloch *opinion, held that laws must be "plainly adapted" to constitutional ends—that is, directly and obviously related to one of Congress's legitimate goals. The "means-ends rationality" test*

Clarence Thomas, concurring opinion, *Sabri v. United States*, U.S. Supreme Court, May 17, 2004.

proposed by Souter greatly extends the traditional meaning of the necessary and proper clause of the Constitution, Thomas maintains.

Title 18 U.S.C. Section 666(a)(2) is a valid exercise of Congress' power to regulate commerce, at least under this Court's precedent. I continue to doubt that we have correctly interpreted the Commerce Clause. But until this Court reconsiders its precedents, and because neither party requests us to do so here, our prior case law controls the outcome of this case.

The Necessary and Proper Clause

I write further because I find questionable the scope the Court gives to the Necessary and Proper Clause as applied to Congress' authority to spend. In particular, the Court appears to hold that the Necessary and Proper Clause authorizes the exercise of any power that is no more than a "rational means" to effectuate one of Congress' enumerated powers. This conclusion derives from the Court's characterization of the seminal case *McCulloch v. Maryland* (1819), as having established a "means-ends rationality" test, a characterization that I am not certain is correct.

In *McCulloch* [referred to in other opinions as *M'Culloch*], the Court faced the question whether the United States had the power to incorporate a national bank. The Court was forced to navigate between the one extreme of the "absolute necessity" construction advocated by the State of Maryland, which would "clog and embarrass" the execution of the enumerated powers "by withholding the most appropriate means" for its execution, and the other extreme, an interpretation that would destroy the Framers' purpose of establishing a National Government of limited and enumerated powers. The Court, speaking through Chief Justice [John] Marshall, carefully and effectively refuted Maryland's proposed "absolute necessity" test. "It must have been the intention of those who gave these powers, to insure, as far as human prudence could insure, their beneficial execution," the Court stated; "[t]his could not be done by confiding the choice of means to such narrow limits as not to leave it in the power of Congress to adopt any which might be appropriate, and which were conducive to the end." The Court opined that it would render the Constitution "a splendid bauble" if "the right to legislate on that vast mass of incidental powers which must be involved in the constitution" were not within the power of Congress.

Proper Use of Federal Power

But the Court did not then conclude that the Necessary and Proper Clause gives unrestricted power to the Federal Government. Rather, it set forth the following test:

> Let the end be legitimate, let it be within the scope of the constitution, and all means which are appropriate, which are plainly adapted to that end, which are not prohibited, but consist with the letter and spirit of the constitution, are constitutional.

"[A]ppropriate" and "plainly adapted" are hardly synonymous with "means-end rationality." Indeed, "plain" means "evident to the mind or senses: *obvious*," "*clear*," and "characterized by simplicity: not complicated [according to various dictionaries Thomas cites]." A statute can have a "rational" connection to an enumerated power without being obviously or clearly tied to that enumerated power. To show that a statute is "plainly adapted" to a legitimate end, then, one must seemingly show more than that a particular statute is a "rational means," to safeguard that end; rather, it would seem necessary to show some obvious, simple, and direct relation between the statute and the enumerated power.

Under the *McCulloch* formulation, I have doubts that Section 666(a)(2) is a proper use of the Necessary and Proper

Clause as applied to Congress' power to spend. Section 666 states that, for any "organization, government, or agency [that] receives, in any one year period, benefits in excess of $10,000 under a Federal program," any person who

> corruptly gives, offers, or agrees to give anything of value to any person, with intent to influence or reward an agent of [such] organization or of [such] State, local or Indian tribal government, or any agency thereof, in connection with any business, transaction, or series of transactions of such organization, government, or agency involving anything of value of $5,000 or more,

commits a federal crime. All that is necessary for Section 666(a)(2) to apply is that the organization, government, or agency in question receives more than $10,000 in federal benefits of any kind, and that an agent of the entity is bribed regarding a substantial transaction of that entity. No connection whatsoever between the corrupt transaction and the federal benefits need be shown.

No Plain Connection Is Required

The Court does a not-wholly-unconvincing job of tying the broad scope of Section 666(a)(2) to a federal interest in federal funds and programs. But simply noting that "[m]oney is fungible," for instance, does not explain how there could be any federal interest in "prosecut[ing] a bribe paid to a city's meat inspector in connection with a substantial transaction just because the city's parks department had received a federal grant of $10,000." It would be difficult to describe the chain of inferences and assumptions in which the Court would have to indulge to connect such a bribe to a federal interest in any federal funds or programs as being "plainly adapted" to their protection. And, this is just one example of many in which any federal interest in protecting federal funds is equally attenuated, and yet the bribe is covered by the expansive language of Section 666(a)(2). Overall, then, Section 666(a)(2) appears to be no more plainly adapted to protecting federal funds or federally funded programs than a hypothetical federal statute criminalizing fraud of any kind perpetrated on any individual who happens to receive federal welfare benefits.

Because I would decide this case on the Court's Commerce Clause jurisprudence, I do not ultimately decide whether Congress' power to spend combined with the Necessary and Proper Clause could authorize the enactment of Section 666(a)(2). But regardless of the particular outcome of this case under the correct test, the Court's approach seems to greatly and improperly expand the reach of Congress' power under the Necessary and Proper Clause.

"The Federal Government can act 'to safeguard the integrity' of grant recipients in order to protect the disbursed funds."

Sabri Shows the Supreme Court's Concern with Corruption

George D. Brown

George D. Brown is the Robert Drinan, S.J., Professor of Law at Boston College Law School. He is a specialist in federal-state relations and government ethics.

The Sabri v. United States (2004) case went against the trend of recent years in backing the national government against the sphere of activity of lower level governments, argues Brown in the following extract. Brown holds that the Court saw the need for integrity in federal programs. Corruption in one area of a local government could signal problems elsewhere, so Congress has a legitimate constitutional interest in allowing the federal government to prosecute local government officials, even if their crimes did not directly involve federal dollars.

The Court's opinion [in *Sabri v. United States*] is a model of simplicity. First of all, Congress had unquestioned authority to appropriate federal grant funds to further the general welfare. Although the Court did not refer to the facts at hand on this point, the housing and other grants received by Minneapolis are typical examples of [congressional] spending

George D. Brown, "Carte Blanche: Federal Prosecution of State and Local Officials After *Sabri*," *Catholic University Law Review*, vol. 54, 2004, pp. 403, 427–30, 432–34. Copyright © 2006 The CUA Law Review Association. Reproduced by permission.

power in action. Second, Congress has "corresponding authority under the Necessary and Proper Clause, to see to it that taxpayer dollars appropriated under [the spending] power are in fact spent for the general welfare, and not frittered away." Congress could well be concerned that dishonest public officers who are "untrustworthy stewards" or who "do not deliver dollar-for-dollar value" will not distinguish according to the source of funds when committing their corrupt acts. Furthermore, the fungibility [interchangeability] of federal funds is an additional reason for not requiring proof of their presence in any particular corrupt activity. The Court invoked Justice [John] Marshall's venerable hypothetical in *McCulloch* [*v. Maryland* (1819)] to the effect that the "power to establish post-offices and post-roads entails authority to punish those who steal letters." [*McCulloch* established Federal authority to operate banks without state taxation or interference.]

The Integrity Rationale

The Court's short and simple analysis almost masks the fact that it adopted one of the major contending arguments in the ongoing debate over the constitutionality of section 666 [of the U.S. Code]: the integrity rationale. The rationale proceeds on the assumption that measures directed solely at transactions involving federal funds will often be insufficient to protect those funds. What is needed is a broad net that achieves protection through sweeping up *all* corrupt transactions in order to guarantee the integrity of the recipient entity. However, this rationale can readily extend to treating the concern for state and local integrity as the major federal interest, with the protection of federal funds operating almost as a pretext. Federalism concerns were barely mentioned in *Sabri*. The Court relegated any problems stemming from "federal prosecution in an area historically of state concern" to a footnote. It found [*United States v.*] *Lopez* [1995] and *United States v. Morrison* (2000) totally inapplicable because those Commerce Clause cases involved activity that had little relation to economic conduct that Congress could regulate.[1] Here, there was no need to "'pile inference upon inference'" since the spending power was directly involved. In sum, whatever constitutional reservations the debate over Section 666 had previously engendered and had come to light in *Salinas* [*v. United States* (1997)] were summarily rejected. After *Sabri*, Section 666 seems free to roam the political landscape as long as the subnational entity where it comes into play receives more than $10,000 in federal funds "'in any one year,'" and the corrupt transaction involves more than $5,000 or, in the Court's words, "goes well beyond liquor and cigars." . . .

The central constitutional aspect of *Sabri* is its acceptance of the integrity rationale, that is, that the Federal Government can act "to safeguard the integrity" of grant recipients in order to protect the disbursed funds. Obviously, integrity might have several meanings. The term might be limited to the federal funds themselves or to the broader manner in which a particular federally funded program is administered. For example, in *Salinas*, correction officials took bribes to permit conjugal visits to federal prisoners housed in a state jail. Integrity might mean the fiscal honesty of a recipient unit as a whole. Again, one can see a tie, albeit less direct, to the federal funds. However, integrity will certainly bear a much broader reading: the general quality of a recipient unit, in the case of a governmental one, whether or not it practices "good government." One could surely find a lack of integrity in a governmental unit in which nepotism and patronage are rampant, "no-show" jobs exist, opposition parties are squelched by entrenched officeholders and there is a general sense of helplessness on the part of excluded groups. Would the *Sabri* rationale permit the Federal Government to regulate these practices directly, for example, by penalizing the awarding of patronage

---

1. Both *Lopez* and *Morrison* struck down certain federal gun control laws as being beyond the Congress's powers enumerated in the Constitution.

jobs? Ultimately there could be a relation back to some federal funds (in the sense that administrative positions with control over those funds might not be awarded on merit), but the goal of federal intervention seems to be the use of the spending power to achieve broader federal public policy ends of good government. . . .

A Case Comparison

At this point, it is instructive to compare *Sabri* with *McConnell [v. Federal Election Commission* (2003)]. *McConnell* upheld restrictions on campaign finance practices and related activities, restrictions that could be enforced through the criminal law. The restrictions were imposed by Congress in the Bipartisan Campaign Reform Act of 2002 (BCRA). BCRA increased the level of regulation of federal campaigns in two primary ways. It sharply curtailed the role of soft money—contributions to political parties for purposes other than the direct influencing of a national election. BCRA also imposed substantial limits on "issue ads," defined by the Court as ads "specifically intended to affect election results," but omitting "'magic words' such as 'Elect John Smith,' or 'Vote against Jane Doe.'" Opponents mounted a substantial First Amendment challenge to BCRA, but a majority of the Court built upon the line of cases beginning with *Buckley v. Valeo* [1976], and amplified in later precedent such as *Nixon v. Shrink Missouri Government PAC*,[2] to formulate a set of anti-corruption governmental interests that met the Government's burden to justify incursions on the First Amendment. The government interest goes beyond preventing quid pro quo [exchanging "this for that"] corruption to countering "the appearance or perception of corruption," and even "'to the broader threat from politicians too compliant with the wishes of large contributors.'"

2. In both *Buckley v. Valeo* and *Nixon v. Shrink Missouri Government PAC*, the Court upheld restrictions on campaign contributions at the federal and state levels, respectively.

One can, of course, identify differences between the two cases. In *McConnell*, the statute regulated the electoral process. In *Sabri*, the statute regulated the functioning of government. *McConnell* involved the regulation of activities primarily at the federal level. *Sabri* involved the regulation of activities at the local level. In *McConnell*, the regulated activities were essentially political advocacy and political contributions. In *Sabri*, the regulated activity was bribery. In *McConnell*, the principal constitutional defense against the challenged statute was the First Amendment. In *Sabri*, the challenge was based on federalism. Finally, *McConnell* relied substantially on notions of public confidence and the appearance of impropriety. *Sabri* focused substantially on the integrity of governmental operations.

The Anti-Corruption Imperative

Despite these differences, I see the two cases united by a broad anti-corruption imperative that justifies Congress's role as the guardian of the democratic process at all stages and at all levels. Each case focused on the importance of integrity in government. The integrity of recipient governments is the key to *Sabri*'s protection of federal funds rationale. *McConnell* invoked prior precedents as demonstrating a congressional intent in protecting "'the integrity of our system of representative democracy.'" As in *Sabri*, the notion of "integrity" is central to the analysis. Indeed, parts of *McConnell* point in a "good government" direction. Beyond a similar approach to recognizing Congress's role in achieving good government, each case demonstrates considerable deference to Congress in determining how to achieve that goal, even in the face of serious constitutional objection.

> *"Focusing on a more direct connection between federal money and illegal activity . . . would ensure that, should Congress decide to criminalize other local conduct . . . a true federal interest will have attached."*

Suggestions to Safeguard Local Control from *Sabri's* Effects

Philip M. Schreiber

Philip M. Schreiber, a 2006 graduate of the American University College of Law, is an attorney with O'Melveny and Myers in Washington, D.C.

Almost all local, state, county, and tribal governments receive federal funds in amounts greater than ten thousand dollars. This means that under 18 U.S. Code, Section 666 (2)(a), virtually all corruption can be a federal crime under the Sabri v. United States (2004) decision, according to Schreiber. If put into widespread practice, Section 666 (2)(a) could be destructive to the U. S. tradition of federalism, the division of government among the national, state, and local levels. To avoid this situation, Schreiber suggests, among other measures, that only local officials who deal with funds—preferably federal funds—should be subject to prosecution under Section 666 (2)(a).

One danger in *Sabri* [*v. United States* (2004)], which the Court seemed to overlook, is that the opinion does not meaningfully curtail the possibility that Congress may use its

Philip M. Schreiber, "Accepting a New Genre of Federal Criminal Laws? How the Supreme Court's Decision in *Sabri* Increases Avenues of Congressional Authority Without Providing Adequate Safeguards for States and Individuals," *Widener Law Review*, vol. 12, 2005–2006, pp. 604–10. Copyright © 2005–2006 Widener University School of Law. Reproduced by permission.

spending powers to increase the number of *other* related federal criminal statutes—actions state laws concomitantly proscribe. The only constitutional limitations on the proliferation of these statutes are: (1) the deferential *McCulloch* [*v. Maryland* (1819)] language, which states that Congress can use the Necessary and Proper Clause [of the Constitution] for any "appropriate," "plainly adapted . . . end" that furthers other constitutionally-vested powers; and (2) the monetary threshold amounts.

No Limits to Federal Intervention

Although the Provision contains two expressed statutory thresholds that arguably ensure a federal interest, the federal interest has been defined as so little that almost nothing would preclude a lower threshold limitation. In other words, of the $51.8 million that Minneapolis received [in the *Sabri* case], what made the $10,000 significant enough in the eyes of the Court such that a federal interest attached? That percentage, approximately 0.02%, is so small that it is not a cognizable barometer or a legally workable threshold that future courts can apply. By "legally workable threshold test," this article means to ask, what quantum of federal funding needs to be at risk in order for *Sabri's* precedent to be applicable? The Supreme Court in this case clearly announced that a $10,000 infusion of federal money into any sub-national governmental entity suffices to create a federal interest. Nevertheless, that limit fails to provide any indication as an answer to the question, how low can Congress go? Congress can rest assured that the Court would uphold any higher threshold. But, if $10,000 a year suffices, does $5,000 a year meet the grade? What about $1,000? Or, $250 a year?

Because *Sabri* failed to establish a "floor" regarding what types of strictures ensure the constitutional validity of a nonconditional, Spending Clause statute, the only indication of what is actually required must be drawn from *Sabri* itself. In

Sabri, the Court interpreted the federal interest broadly; if Congress deemed it worthy, it could pass a multitude of laws based on the *Sabri* rationale (alleged protection of federal disbursements) that create federal criminal jurisdiction for other actions that may threaten federal disbursements in one form or another.

Under *Sabri*'s underlying principle, individuals may face federal charges for simple intrastate crimes passed under the Spending Clause, such as burglarizing the home of an individual if the victim is a welfare beneficiary or a beneficiary of any other federal program regarding the property. This position was adopted by the Government at oral argument in response to the logical ends of the Provision's constitutional underpinnings. The *Sabri* rationale applies because the connection between the federal interest at issue in some of the more far-fetched section 666 cases is just as attenuated as the interest the federal government could claim in securing these homes. For example, in some section 666 cases, the alleged federal interest is not in the federal money itself, but rather a weakness in a "sister" state program, which in turn receives federal money, and is several layers removed from federal disbursements. In the hypothetical, the federal interest is similar: providing someone with federal money—a home loan or welfare benefits—and ensuring that this money is not lost or wasted because of criminal activity. . . .

A Universe of Federalized Crime

The Court's determination that Congress has a sufficient federal interest in safeguarding its funds, and therefore can criminalize a universe of local, unrelated conduct, assumes that the threat produced by a corrupt official somewhere in the branch of government will always threaten to cause a siphoning and waste of funds somewhere else in the system. The Court disregards the fact that sub-national governments may have separate, disconnected spheres. An agent who takes a bribe on one end does not necessarily have any effect on commingled funds (or threaten those funds) on the other end.

The Court essentially contended that a sub-national government is entirely interconnected and watered with revenue by largess, tax proceeds, and other revenue-raising activities. The deluge of government largess and taxes is all the same—it is fungible and liquid. Thus, the sustenance it gets from federal disbursements is commingled and indistinguishable from that which it receives from state sources and tax revenues.

If a corrupt public servant accepts a bribe and either directly or indirectly diverts money from one recipient to another (again, it does not matter if it is state money or federal money, because they are commingled), then the diversion of resources is at the cost of the remainder of the government. In effect, the Court assumed it is a zero-sum game; the government must reroute resources from other areas to cover what is being lost on one end.

Although this may seem like a sensible analysis of how corruption and bribery affect resource allocation, the reality of state or local government structure does not necessarily lend itself to so simple a construct. Nevertheless, this is essentially the system of government the *Sabri* Court presupposed when it upheld section 666.

There is no doubt that there are many cases, like in *Sabri*, where the connection between a federal grant and a corrupt government agent directly or indirectly would cause waste. However, the hypothetical posed and the various cases cited demonstrate that there are many instances where no connection exists between federal disbursements and local corruption.

Some Suggestions

Obviously, no single example is perfect. They are used to illustrate that the "one-size-fits-all" approach, which the government proffered and to which the *Sabri* Court subscribed, should have, in light of principles of federalism, been subject to increased scrutiny by the Court.

A more proper approach that balances the needs and desires of Congress with federalism is for Congress to require the government to prove an additional element in its section 666 cases: (1) that section 666 apply only to specific programs actually receiving funds from a federal source; (2) that the recipient, or would-be recipient, of the bribe be in an authoritative and controlling position over either federal, state, or local money; or (3) in response to an illicit quid pro quo exchange, federal, state, or local money was in fact siphoned off from one department to another in order to cover a loss.

The first element would limit the scope of federal prosecutors' ability to prosecute a corrupt town property assessor because the town's public hospital was in receipt of $10,001 of Medicare benefits. By contrast, the government would be able to bring a less disjointed case if, for example, the town obtained a federal grant from the Census Bureau (which is seeking a determination of average home values) *and* the property assessor was involved in a bribery scheme.

The second element would ensure that at the very least the individual was in a position where he or she could directly affect funding in the future, even if the bribe failed to influence any money whatsoever. This threat seemed to be a central reason why Congress passed section 666.

The last suggested element would, of course, be the most difficult to prove. However, it is a recommendation of last resort, as the first two proposals balance the requirements of federalism with the needs of safeguarding public funding.

Any one of these additional statutory elements would satisfy the government's federal interest—protecting federal money, or federal money that is so commingled with other revenue sources as to be indistinguishable from the remainder of the sub-national government's income stream. Further, this would more closely bring non-conditional Spending Clause laws in-line with the Court's Commerce Clause and conditional Spending Clause precedents.

Additionally, they would do so without federally criminalizing the conduct of individuals who: (1) have no direct connection to federal money by virtue of being in a completely different department than one that receives funding; (2) have no authority over money, deeming them a non-threat to the overall system; or (3) fail to affect the allocation of the overall pool of resources. A solution to parrying the thrust of future non-conditional, federal criminal statutes would require detailed information of the statute itself. Suffice it to say that these types of checks—focusing on a more direct connection between federal money and illegal activity—would ensure that, should Congress decide to criminalize other local conduct under its Spending Clause, a true federal interest will have attached.

Organizations to Contact

The editors have compiled the following list of organizations concerned with the issues debated in this book. The descriptions are derived from materials provided by the organizations. All have publications or information available for interested readers. The list was compiled on the date of publication of the present volume; the information provided here may change. Be aware that many organizations take several weeks or longer to respond to inquiries, so allow as much time as possible.

Brookings Institution
1775 Massachusetts Ave. NW, Washington, DC   20036
(202) 797-6000
e-mail: communications@brookings.edu
Web site: www.brookings.edu

The Brookings Institution is a long-established, center/left-leaning think tank. It publishes extensively on various issues, including governmental corruption.

Campaign Disclosure Project
California Voter Foundation, Sacramento, CA   95816
(916) 441-2494
e-mail: will@calvoter.org
Web site: www.campaigndisclosure.org

The Campaign Disclosure Project is a joint initiative of the University of California, Los Angeles (UCLA) School of Law, the Center for Governmental Studies, and the California Voter Foundation. It works to highlight the role of money in political campaigns at the state and federal level and to increase the transparency of campaign finance. Its Web site features a "Campaign Finance Disclosure Model Law" designed to serve as a guide for legislators in devising financial regulations for election campaigns as well as a database of state financial disclosure laws.

Campaign Finance Institute (CFI)
1990 M Street NW, Suite 380, Washington, DC   20036
(202) 969-8890
e-mail: info@cfinst.org
Web site: www.cfinst.org

This scholarly organization, affiliated with the George Washington University, publishes studies on the effects of campaign finance laws. Its Web site is a valuable source of information on the laws themselves. Recent publications, available on the Web site, include "Rethinking the Campaign Finance Agenda" by Michael J. Malbin and various press releases analyzing spending in recent elections.

Cato Institute
1000 Massachusetts Ave. NW, Washington, DC   20001-5403
(202) 842-0200
Web site: www.cato.org

The Cato Institute is a libertarian think tank. Its publications show a special concern with issues of federalism and increasing centralization of power in Washington. Its reports and opinion columns, available on its Web site, have been critical of the federal government's increased role in prosecuting local government corruption.

Federal Bureau of Investigation (FBI)
J. Edgar Hoover Building, Washington, DC   20535
(202) 324-3000
Web site: www.fbi.gov

The Federal Bureau of Investigation is the national agency in charge of investigating political corruption involving the federal government. Congressional legislation has expanded the bureau's role, enabling it to investigate corruption in any local government that receives federal money, meaning virtually all municipalities and counties in the United States. More information can be found at its public corruption Web page.

Global Integrity
1029 Vermont Ave. NW, Suite 600, Washington, DC   20005
(202) 449-4100
e-mail: info@globalintegrity.org
Web site: www.globalintegrity.org

Global Integrity monitors political corruption worldwide. One of the features of its Web site is a blog, commons.globalintegrity.org, which features current news on corruption-related issues around the world. The organization also publishes yearly scorecards, rating countries on their anticorruption activities.

Hoover Institution
434 Galvez Mall, Stanford, CA   94305-6010
toll-free: (877) 466-8374
e-mail: oishi@hoover.stanford.edu
Web site: www.hoover.org

Generally considered to be on the conservative side of the political spectrum, the Hoover Institution is one of the nation's top think tanks. It hosts scholars researching campaign finance laws and their effects. Its Campaign Finance site contains both original research and links to articles on campaign reform as well as a useful time line of campaign finance laws and a glossary of relevant terms.

Transparency International USA
1023 Fifteenth St. NW, Suite 300, Washington, DC   20005
(202) 589-1616
e-mail: administration@transparency-usa.org
Web site: www.transparency-usa.org

This organization is the U.S. branch of Transparency International. The group fights for good governance worldwide, focusing especially on bribery and links between corporations and governments. Its Web site features a large number of links to reports on corruption, as well as an "anti-bribery toolkit" to help small and medium-size businesses avoid becoming victims of corrupt practices.

U.S. Office of Governmental Ethics (OGE)
1201 New York Ave. NW, Suite 500, Washington, DC   20005
(202) 482-9300
e-mail: contactOGE@oge.gov
Web site: www.usoge.gov

Established by the Ethics in Government Act of 1978, the main mission of the U.S. Office of Governmental Ethics is to prevent conflicts of interest involving federal government employees. The site is also a key source of current anticorruption law, rules, and regulations.

For Further Research

Books

Floyd Abrams, *Speaking Freely: Trials of the First Amendment*. New York: Viking Penguin, 2005.

Kenneth D. Ackerman, *Boss Tweed: The Rise and Fall of the Corrupt Pol Who Conceived the Soul of Modern New York*. New York: Carroll & Graf, 2006.

Anthony Corrado, *The New Campaign Finance Sourcebook*. Washington, DC: Brookings Institution Press, 2005.

Thomas J. Craughwell and M. William Phelps, *Failures of the Presidents: From the Whiskey Rebellion and War of 1812 to the Bay of Pigs and War in Iraq*. Beverly, MA: Fair Winds Press, 2008.

Lanny J. Davis, *Scandal: How "Gotcha" Politics Is Destroying America*. New York: Palgrave Macmillan, 2006.

W. Mark Felt and John O'Connor, *A G-Man's Life: The FBI, Being "Deep Throat," and the Struggle for Honor in Washington*. 1st ed. New York: Public Affairs, 2006.

Jack Germond, *Fat Man Fed Up: How American Politics Went Bad*. New York: Random House, 2004.

Steven M. Gillon, *"That's Not What We Meant to Do": Reform and Its Unintended Consequences in Twentieth-Century America*. New York: Norton, 2000.

Louis Patrick Gray and Ed Gray, *In Nixon's Web: A Year in the Crosshairs of Watergate*. New York: Henry Holt, 2008.

Gerald S. Greenberg, *Historical Encyclopedia of U.S. Independent Counsel Investigations*. Westport, CT: Greenwood, 2000.

Mark Grossman, *Political Corruption in America: An Encyclopedia of Scandals, Power, and Greed*. Millerton, NY: Grey House, 2008.

Arianna Stassinopoulos Huffington, *Pigs at the Trough: How Corporate Greed and Political Corruption Are Undermining America*. New York: Crown, 2003.

Gerald E. Kelly, *Honor for Sale*. New York: Sharon, 1999.

Kim Long, *The Almanac of Political Corruption, Scandals, and Dirty Politics*. New York: Delacorte, 2007.

Michael J. Malbin, *The Election After Reform: Money, Politics, and the Bipartisan Campaign Reform Act; Campaigning American Style*. Lanham, MD: Rowman & Littlefield, 2006.

Greg Palast, *The Best Democracy Money Can Buy: An Investigative Reporter Exposes the Truth About Globalization, Corporate Cons, and High Finance Fraudsters*. Sterling, VA: Pluto, 2002.

Christopher H. Schroeder et al., *Presidential Power Stories*. New York: Foundation Press, 2009.

Bradley A. Smith, *Unfree Speech: The Folly of Campaign Finance Reform*. Princeton, NJ: Princeton University Press, 2001.

Rodney A. Smith, *Money, Power and Elections: How Campaign Finance Reform Subverts American Democracy*. Baton Rouge: Louisiana State University Press, 2006.

Kathleen Tracy, *The Watergate Scandal*. Hockessin, DE: Mitchell Lane, 2007.

Larry A. Van Meter, *United States v. Nixon: The Question of Executive Privilege*. New York: Chelsea House, 2006.

Periodicals

Jonathan Alter, "If Watergate Happened Now," *Newsweek*, July 13, 2005.

Timothy J. Burger and Brian Bennett, "The FBI Gets Tough," *Time*, January 23, 2006.

Eliza Newlin Carney, "The Anti-Reformers," *National Journal*, February 17, 2001.

Christian Science Monitor, "Yet Another Counsel," May 15, 1998.

Julian A. Cook III, "The Independent Counsel Statute: A Premature Demise," *Brigham Young University Law Review*, December 1999.

David Corn, "Not-So-Special Counsel," *Nation*, February 2, 2004.

Economist, "Are Independent Counsels Necessary?" March 6, 1999.

———, "It's Corruption, Stupid," January 7, 2006.

Joshua Green, "Schools for Scandal," *Atlantic Monthly*, March 2006.

Mark Hansen, "Anything but Typical: *McConnell v. FEC*," *ABA Journal*, September 2003.

Christopher Hayes, "Corruption—a Proven Winner," *Nation*, May 2, 2005.

Charles F. Hinkle, "Can Campaign Finance Reform Coexist with the First Amendment?" *Human Rights*, Winter 1998.

Reynolds Holding, "The Executive Privilege Showdown," *Time*, March 21, 2007.

Human Events, "So, Now They Want a Special Counsel," October 6, 2003.

Tena Jamison Lee, "A Pro and Con Debate: How Much Campaign Finance Reform Do We Need?" *Human Rights*, Winter 1998.

New Republic, "Good Riddance," July 5, 1999.

P.J. O'Rourke, "Incumbent-Protection Acts," *Atlantic Monthly*, April 2005.

Matthew Robinson, "Campaign Finance: No There, There," *Human Events*, January 22, 2001.

Andrew Romano, "Watergate Revisited: Following Felt's Trail," *Newsweek*, June 13, 2005.

Terence Samuel, "McCain & Co. Win Campaign Finance Bout," *U.S. News & World Report*, April 9, 2001.

Bradley A. Smith, "The Gaggers and Gag-Making," *National Review*, March 11, 2002.

Alexandra Starr and Richard S. Dunham, "Campaign-Finance Reform Only a Republican Could Love?" *BusinessWeek*, April 21, 2003.

John Stossel, "Big Government Means Corruption," *Human Events*, January 5, 2009.

Paul Taylor, "The Short, Unhappy Life of Campaign Finance Reform," *Mother Jones*, March 2003.

USA Today (magazine), "Independent Counsel Bills Bleeding Taxpayers Dry," August 1998.

Internet Sources

Alafair Burke, "The New, New Federalism? *Sabri v. United States*," *Findlaw.com*, December 11, 2003. http://writ.news.findlaw.com.

The Clairmont Institute, "Let the Independent Counsel Law Die," February 22, 1999. www.claremont.org.

Gary Lawson, "Making a Federal Case Out of It: *Sabri v. United States* and the Constitution of Leviathan," *Cato Supreme Court Review 2003–2004*, 2004. www.cato.org.

Jason J. Vicente, "Impeachment, a Constitutional Primer," *Policy Analysis*, no. 318, September 18, 1998. www.cato.org.

George Will, "The Incumbent Protection Act," *Pittsburgh Tribune*, November 25, 2007. www.pittsburghlive.com.

Index